Riding Babyface

Riding Babyface

By

Wanda Snow Porter

To Babyface

Chapter One
Summer~1957

Goodbye Cottonwillow Union Elementary. I won't miss you.

I took one last look at the tan plastered building. Hooray, I made it. I'd graduated from eighth grade. I clutched my diploma, turned, and hurried to catch up with Mama and Daddy.

When we got home, as I always did after school, I changed from my dress to jeans and went out to the corral. My horse, Billy, was a good listener, and while I groomed his summer coat to a luster, I told him about my graduation.

Because of his huge head and enormous height, we never found a saddle or bridle big enough to fit him. So I tied a rope around his nose, used the rail of the fence to climb on, and rode him bareback along the endless roads crisscrossing our cotton farm. The old workhorse didn't hurry, no matter how much I kicked. His super-sized round feet weighed a ton. When the homely brown giant walked, he dragged them and furrowed wide hoof prints on the dusty road.

After my ride, I hurriedly brushed Billy. Then I went into the house, washed my hands, and helped Mama set the dinner table. As we piled our plates with chicken, I asked, "Daddy, for a graduation gift, can I get a new horse? One that gallops."

"Horses, horses, horses." Mama shook her head. "You sound like a broken record."

"How can I ever become a trainer riding a horse who falls asleep while Veronica shows off and does handstands on his rump? Without a livelier horse, I'll never learn the first thing about training."

"You couldn't ride a more spirited horse," Veronica said, then looked at me with a smirk.

I ignored my sister's nasty remark and said, "As soon as I save enough money, I'm going to order *Professor Beery's Mail Course in Horsemanship Training Manual* I saw advertised in the newspaper."

Daddy cleared his throat. Everyone stared at him as he looked intently at Mama. "I found a small apple farm on the California coast for sale. I want us to buy it." He paused a moment and then said, "The weather is cooler there. I've survived the Depression, droughts, and dust storms, but don't think I can tolerate another hot Bakersfield summer."

It was 1957, but Daddy still talked about the Great Depression. His dark hair showed little gray, which gave him the appearance of a man too young to have been born years before 1929.

Mama frowned. "With your diabetes acting up the way it is, you need to take it easy, not buy an apple orchard out in the country. We should move into town, closer to the doctors."

Daddy adamantly shook his head. "I'd hate living in town. The apple farm isn't far out. It's only about a mile from Arroyo Viejo."

"It would be serious if your sugar level gets out of whack. You've got to think of your health." Mama crumpled her napkin and threw it on her plate. She stood and began to clear the table.

Was Daddy's diabetes getting worse? He never acted sick, always cheerful and joking. With Mama's pessimistic I-got-up-on-the-wrong-side-of-the-bed attitude, she always made the smallest worry seem like an immense catastrophe.

After a week of expressing all her worries, Mama agreed to move to the coast.

The worst thing about moving was we couldn't find a horse trailer big enough to tote Billy. When I learned Daddy sold him to a neighbor, an ache filled my chest, and I started bawling. Billy was my best friend.

I'd been horse-crazy since fourth grade. That's when I went to the circus and saw a woman wearing a blue-plumed turban and pink tights perform acrobatic feats on a galloping pure white stallion. After her act, a group of beautiful Arabians entered the big tent. I closed my eyes and imagined I stood in the center ring wearing high black boots and a red top hat and tailcoat, circled by the five golden steeds.

Ever since then, when Mama drank and things got awful, I'd dream of running away to the circus to become the protégé of the star horse performer.

A few days before we moved, Daddy and I led Billy to his new home. A clean stall with a manger full of hay awaited his arrival. "Good-bye, Billy. I love you. I'll miss you forever," I said and wrapped my arms around the old horse's massive neck, hugged him, and sobbed.

On the walk home, I sniveled and wiped my tears on my sleeve. Daddy put his arm around my shoulders and promised to buy another horse once we got settled in our new home.

On moving day, two men loaded a large Mayflower van with our furniture. After the movers left, we all piled into our black Buick. Puppy, our dog, jumped in the back seat with my sister and me. I looked out the car's rear window as we left our driveway to travel toward new neighbors and a house I'd never seen.

We rolled down all the car's windows to let the warm breeze cool us. Cotton planted in long rows and fields of alfalfa turned the desert green, and the hot, humid air smelled like newly mown hay. The ghostly, wavy images rising from the black asphalt gave the trip a dream-like quality.

When we got closer to the coast, the road became so curvy Puppy got carsick and upchucked on the floor. Mama was whopping mad, and Daddy wasn't too happy, either. We stopped at a gas station and got paper towels out of the bathroom to clean up the mess, but the car still had a nasty dog-puke smell even though the windows were all rolled down.

About the time the dog-vomit stink aired out of the Buick, we came to an orchard of leafy green apple trees planted in neat rows. We turned off the main road onto a long dirt driveway that ended at an old red farmhouse with white trim.

By the time we arrived, the movers had just finished unloading our furniture. Puppy and I leaped out of the car, greeted by the sweet smell of a honeysuckle vine that climbed on a trellis by the front door. Calla lilies grew next to the house, scattered around as if Mother Nature had planted them.

Puppy trotted up steps that went up a hill behind the house. As I began to climb them to explore, Mama yelled, "Winna, don't wander off. I need you to help carry boxes."

I skulked back to carry in a heavy box of records from the trunk of our car. Elvis was my favorite singer, and we had all of his 45s. As I walked by the front bedroom Veronica had dibbed, she hollered, "Hey, bring those in here."

I detoured into her room. She sat on her unmade bed with her long legs crossed at the ankles like a princess on a throne. My sister was tall and pretty with dark brown hair and hazel eyes like Daddy's. She was a better horseback rider than I was but didn't care much about horses. Boys were her main interest. She always had a boyfriend.

Me, I was short, had blue eyes, hair the color of straw, loved horses, and thought boys were pains. Mama said I favored Daddy's mother. I looked so different from my parents and sister. Sometimes I felt I was left as a baby on the doorstep by a musical troupe of Swedish gypsies.

Veronica pointed at a place on her desk next to a portable record player where I was supposed to set the records. "Watch out! Don't drop them. You'll die if you break one."

"Maybe you could help," I grumbled, placing the box on the desk.

"Be careful of *my* records and *my* record player." Veronica jutted her chin, pursed her lips into a tight little zero, and gave me an ornery glare.

"Mama said I could use the record player."

"But only when *I* say." Grasping my shoulder, she shoved me out of her bedroom. "Remember, my room is off-limits. Don't come in unless I say so."

I screamed, "You're a nasty snot rag." I hated when my sister treated me like an extra toe with an ingrown toenail. We argued a lot. Half the time, we were best of friends, the other half, the worst of friends. Ours was a sometimes-love-sometimes-hate relationship.

"Stop arguing," Mama hollered from the kitchen.

Even though mad enough to spit, I shut my trap and hauled the rest of my stuff into my room. A tree outside my bedroom window caused the afternoon sunshine to splatter on the bumpy, green walls and rose-patterned linoleum. A brown plywood wardrobe with sliding doors served as a closet. It took up a three-by-four-foot space and made the small room even smaller.

In the kitchen, Mama and Daddy unpacked boxes of dishes the movers had left stacked on the table. I went in to help and asked, "Why does Veronica get the front bedroom? It's way bigger than mine. Why can't I have it? It isn't fair that she gets the biggest room just because she's the oldest."

"Life isn't fair, Winna," Mama said.

She always said that when she really meant "no." However, Mama was right. If life were fair, I'd have a nicer sister, I'd be pretty and smart, and my family would act nice like the Nelsons on the *Ozzie and Harriet* TV show.

Wringing her hands the way she always did when upset, Mama stared out the kitchen window. Then she turned and said to Daddy, "They call this a 'gentleman farm.' Ha. Dusty and dirty, a lot of work, and not much income is what it'll be."

Daddy ignored her complaint and kept unpacking dishes.

A wood-burning stove squatted like a black toad in one corner of the kitchen. Trying to make Veronica jealous, I said, "Oh look, a delightful potbellied stove. With a nice morning fire, my bedroom next to the kitchen will be cozy and warm." I peeked inside a door off the kitchen. "And I'm closer to the bathroom. Dibs on being the first to soak in this gigantic clawfoot tub."

The tiny bathroom wouldn't be a problem because my parents' bath and bedroom were off the screened porch. Mama complained teenage girls were noisy and having our room on the other side of the house would be quieter so Daddy could rest.

"Stop snooping and help put things away."

As usual, Mama sounded exasperated.

After I'd helped her put the dishes away and finished carrying in all the boxes, I checked out the old house's cupboards and closets. It had lots of weird cubbyholes. The kind of places Mama liked to hide her bottles.

On the back porch, a rusty sword sat in the corner of a stale smelling pantry. I returned to the kitchen, waved it, and squealed, "Look what I found."

"Let's see it." Daddy ran his finger down the blade, nodded, and then handed it back to me. "It's a bayonet."

"A what?"

"A bayonet. It attaches to an army rifle for hand-to-hand combat."

"Oh, yeah, like in the war movies." I sliced the air with it, fighting an imagined foe. "Maybe Mr. Buck fought alongside President Eisenhower and stabbed someone with it."

"Quit waving that thing," Mama said. "Eisenhower was a general during the war, too old to fight hand-to-hand combat. Mr. Buck must have forgotten it. Put it back where you found it, and I'll return it to him."

Mama and Daddy were Democrats and didn't vote for Ike. Mama said his Vice President, Richard Nixon, had shifty eyes. On the TV news, with his round, bald head, the president looked like an old elf. It was hard to imagine he was the top general during the war.

Mama turned and pointed at me. "Hurry up! Put the bayonet back, unpack your suitcase, and make your bed."

In my little bedroom, I shook out the sheets, smoothed them and tucked the ends under the mattress. Then I sat on it.

The tree outside filtered light from the sunset into eerie images. Shadows filled the corners. I squeezed my eyes shut and prayed the cooler weather on the coast would make Daddy feel better, and Mama would be happy here and stay sober.

She complained life on the cotton farm was hard and lonely. Her unhappiness made her seem old. It was difficult to believe she was ever young. She was a worrywart, but not the only one. Starting ninth grade at a new school in the fall worried me. High school would be more challenging than grammar school. My sister would be a junior and said ninth was easy. I wasn't so sure.

Besides worrying about bad grades, I wouldn't know anyone except my sister. She said hanging out with her was a definite no-no. Maybe not knowing anyone would be an advantage. If no one knew anything about me, making friends might be easier.

I read somewhere, "To make friends, you've got to be a friend." Except first, I had to make one. It had never been easy to make friends, real ones, not the kind that whispered about your family behind your back.

At my eighth-grade graduation ceremony, our principal said we needed goals and aspirations. So I decided to make a list of mine. I found a pencil and a school notebook in one of the unpacked boxes and wrote out my list in the magnitude of importance.

1. Get a horse
2. Make at least one friend
3. Don't flunk ninth grade
4. Keep Mama happy

After some consideration, so I could achieve goals and aspirations 1, 2, and 3, I changed keeping Mama happy to number 1 on the list.

Chapter Two
The Barn

I pulled on my cut-off jeans, slipped on a shirt, and then peeked into Veronica's room to see if she was awake. Her head was hidden under the covers. I whispered, "Veronica?"

No answer.

I was ready to stomp around the living room to wake her up when, like a flash, she leaped from under the covers and yelled, "Booo."

I jumped back and squealed, "Eeek!"

She lay back on her bed and rolled with giggles.

"It's not funny. I could've died of a heart attack."

"You're too young to have a heart attack, stupid."

"No. You're stupid." The linoleum felt cold under my bare feet as I stuck my foot into her room and touched my big toe inside her territory to test if she was over her mad. When she didn't yell, I stepped inside. "You want to go up the hill and check out the pasture?"

"Sure." Yawning, she leisurely stretched her arms over her head and then sat up.

While she dressed, I went into the kitchen where Mama sat with her elbows on the table, drinking coffee and smoking a cigarette. "Is it okay if we go explore?" I asked.

She frowned at my bare feet. "Ladies wear shoes."

Mama's ladies' list began when I started kindergarten. Showing my underwear became her big concern because I wore dresses to school. Which meant fun things like hanging upside down on the monkey bars wasn't allowed. It was tough sitting with my knees squinched together using muscles otherwise never used. Wearing a dress to school was stupid. I wouldn't have to worry about my undies showing if girls could wear jeans to school.

As I got older, the ladies' list grew. Whenever I did anything Mama deemed unladylike, she added more rules like ladies chew with their mouths shut and never stare or point. It was so boring. Did boys have a gentleman's list?

She took a long drag on the last inch of her cigarette and then squished the butt out in the ashtray. "Stay out of the poison oak. It's all over the hillside. And stay out of that bunkhouse. Mrs. Buck left her antiques in there until she finds a new place to store them." She wagged her finger at me. "Mind me now. Don't get into her things. Besides, the bunkhouse is full of poisonous black widow spiders. Do you understand?"

"Of course, Mama," Veronica said as she entered the kitchen. "We'll only look around to see what's up there. We won't go near Mrs. Buck's antiques."

The cracked and crumbling cement steps turned into a steep dirt trail. We climbed to the top, past the pasture's iron gate where a watering trough stood, shaded by an oak tree. About twenty feet beyond, a small shack stood beside an ancient-looking barn.

I stopped to peer into the trough's stagnate, moss-covered water. "Look, it's alive with polliwogs and frogs."

"Forget that," Veronica said and beelined to the ramshackle building. "Let's see what old Mrs. Buck stored inside the bunkhouse." Weathered and unpainted, about the size of a single-car garage, it was a perfect place to park a Model T.

"Wait!" I said. "Mama said not to go in there."

Veronica paid no attention. "Looks like no one's opened this in years." Dirt had piled up in front of its door, and she struggled with it, determined to see inside. "Come on, help me."

I helped kick dirt away, and we forced the door open to the smell of dust mingled with mildew. Inside, dishes, knickknacks, and all kinds of curious-looking things were piled high, stacked more than halfway up the wall. A cobwebbed path zigzagged through the junk toward the back of the bunkhouse. We gazed inside, but neither of us squeezed in for a closer look.

Veronica spied some odd gadget on top of the pile in the back of the dimly lit shed and pointed. "Gee, what weird stuff. Go in and get that."

"Nope, you go. I'm not going in there with all those spiders. Besides, if Mama catches us snooping in here, we'll be in big trouble. I don't want to do anything to make her mad. She'll tell Daddy not to get me a horse."

"Don't worry. Mama won't come up here. She'll never find out."

"All the same, if you're so interested in antiques, get it yourself."

Veronica poked around in the dusty hodgepodge of oddities closest to the door. She peered further inside but then shrugged. "Nothing in here is worth much."

"Oh, yeah, sure, sure," I said, glad she'd chickened out, not wanting to get in trouble. "Let's see inside the old barn. It'll be perfect for a horse."

Together we shoved the big bunkhouse door shut. To make it appear as if we never opened it, I smoothed the dirt and covered our tracks.

On one side of the barn, a large door stood open. We entered and stepped out of the sunshine into dim light filtered through the spaces between broad slats. Sheltered by the thick beams and old weathered wood, it felt as if a warm cloak of permanence, of safety, surrounded me.

The barn had two sections. On the narrower side, a manger for feeding cows and horses separated the larger part. There, an old tractor sat parked on the other side of bales of hay stacked into a ten-foot-tall step pyramid. Blackened by age, harness hung on rusty nails high along the roof's edge. Everything looked as if it had been abandoned here for years, perhaps forgotten and left behind by someone in a hurry to leave.

Over the haystack, a rope dangled from the barn's high center beam.

"Look," I said. "If we stand on the haystack, we can reach the rope."

"Bet someone got hanged with that rope," Veronica said. "Maybe they're buried right here under our feet."

She knew I was afraid of ghosts. I glanced down and got the creeps. "Quit trying to scare me. That rope isn't like the hanging ropes they use in the cowboy movies. It's way too fat to make a good noose."

In cowboy movies, they chased bad guys and hanged them from a tree limb. The best thing about the movies was the beautiful horses. As famous as Roy Rogers, Trigger was the prettiest palomino in the world. The Cisco Kid's pinto was beautiful too. I couldn't wait to get a horse and gallop around the pasture the way they did in the movies.

Veronica climbed on top of the haystack, reached up to grasp the rope, jumped off the stack, and pushed hard when her feet touched the barn walls. "Maybe no one was hanged," she yelled, "but this is a perfect swinging rope."

I grew impatient waiting for my turn while she swung back and forth, flying from one side of the barn to the other. Sailing through the air looked exciting. Daredevil Veronica made everything look fun. Except, sometimes, her idea of fun got me into trouble and made Mama *very* unhappy.

Chapter Three
Horses

About a week after we moved, Mama insisted I go with her to meet the neighbors. We crossed the road to their house and heard a racket. I followed Mama as she walked to the backyard. A tall, silver-haired man fed carrots into a juicer with carrot pulp piling around his feet like orange sawdust. He saw us and turned off the noisy machine.

"Hello," Mama said. "We just moved in across the street. I'm Sarah Beckman, and this is my daughter Winna."

"Glad to meet you. I'm George Barr. Welcome to the neighborhood." He held out a mason jar filled with orange-colored juice and offered it to Mama. "This will cure you of everything."

"No, thank you," she said.

How did carrot juice taste? I reached out, took the jar, and sipped a tiny sip. Yuck. Warm carrot juice tasted awful. I quickly gave the jar back to him.

"Our garden's gunna have a big tomato crop to can this year. Nothing better than freshly canned vegetables. You like apple jelly?" Mr. Barr opened his garage door. Inside, jars and bottles, big and little, full of red, yellow, and green fruits and vegetables filled shelves that reached the roof.

"I make delicious jelly." He selected two jars and held them out. "Here, have some."

"Thanks. I'm sure we'll enjoy them." Mama's smile made her brown eyes sparkle and softened her usually sour face.

"I make great raspberry wine. I'll get you some." He walked to shelves in the back of the garage. "This is where I keep the good stuff."

Mama shook her head. "No, thank you. We don't drink."

Gads, if he only knew.

"You're missing out. This is great wine."

Mama shook her head again. "I'm sure it is, but no, thank you."

A woman opened the back door of the house and came out on the porch. Her gray hair was pulled into a bun. She wore an apron over her dress and low-heeled, black-laced shoes. "I thought I heard someone talking. Howdy, I'm Eloise. Is that husband of mine trying to tempt you with his homemade wine?" She chuckled. "It's not as good as he says. Come on in."

In her sunny kitchen, an ivy vine grew along the corner of the ceiling. Before I sat down, Mrs. Barr told me, "Go check the berry vines and see if any are ripe. Pick as many as you like."

Outside, I smiled when Mr. Barr pointed at the patch of vegetables alongside the garage. Huge squash plants, tall stalks of corn, and rows of beans grew in his garden. I searched through the vines overloaded with blackberries. I stuffed so many tart-sweet berries in my mouth juice ran down my chin, and I had to use my shirt sleeve as a napkin.

Mama eagle-eyed me when she and Mrs. Barr came outside.

"I'll pick the children up for church around 10:30 if that's okay?" Mrs. Barr said. When she smiled at me, her teeth looked perfect and false. "You'll love our church. Come over any time and enjoy these berries. We grow more than we can use, and you're welcome to them."

On the way home, Mama and I walked by a giant tree growing along Barr's driveway, loaded with cherries. Maybe they needed this tree picked too.

When we were far enough from their house to be out of earshot, Mama squawked, "Your face is a mess, and so's your shirt. Ladies don't use their sleeves to wipe their mouths. Mrs. Barr will think we're bumpkins."

Mama worried since we lived on a farm, people would compare us to the Yokums, characters in the *Li'l Abner* comic strip she loved to read in Sunday's newspaper.

"Don't worry. My chest is too flat. No one will mistake me for Daisy Mae. Besides, the Barrs act more like bumpkins than we do. He makes Kickapoo joy juice, and she dresses like Mammy Yokum." Pulling my shirt out to make large, pointy breasts, I started to giggle.

Mama frowned. "You're not funny."

I bit my lip to stop smiling. "What's this about her taking us to church?"

"She offered to take you. Going to church is good for you."

As usual, Mama used the old for-your-own-good ploy. "Why don't you take us? We could all go," I said.

She shook her head. "You know your daddy doesn't like going to church."

"Well, if church is so good for me, why isn't it good for you and Daddy?"

"You know he says when he's working in the fields and watching things grow, he feels closer to God than when inside a church."

"Well, I don't want to go. I'd rather stay home and feel closer to God with Daddy."

Mama squinted, pinpointing me with her glare. "Quit arguing. It's time you start acting like a young lady. Besides, there's lots of singing. You'll like it. Veronica is going, too. It's kind of Mrs. Barr to take you."

The truth was, Mama wanted to get rid of us on Sunday mornings and didn't want to be bothered to take us to church herself. Lucky for her, Mrs. Barr was a nice neighbor.

When we got home, in the front yard, Veronica stood and watched while Daddy threw a saddle on a golden chestnut mare. A darker version of Trigger, she had a flaxen mane and tail but no socks or stockings or other markings except for a small star centered between her eyes. She was tall, but not nearly as tall as Billy.

I ran up to the mare. Jumping up and down, I squealed, "Where'd you get the horse?"

Daddy latched onto the mare's halter. "Whoa there, Winna. Don't scream. You'll scare the mare."

I quit hopping around, and he grinned down at me. "From a neighbor in the next canyon. I saw a Kid's-Horse-For-Sale sign along the road, so I stopped to look. Won't have to hear any more begging about getting a horse, will I?"

I smiled up at him. Daddy knew everything about horses. Raised on a farm, he drove a team of workhorses to plow the fields. He rode horseback everywhere, even to town. When he grew up, it was like living in the dark ages. But it would have been great riding horses all day.

Daddy said his father didn't get a tractor until right before WWII started. Then the government needed corn, cotton, and wheat. Before that, he said farmers were going broke and leaving their farms to find work. Too young to join the army and go off to war, he stayed on the farm and helped raise crops for the war effort.

He pulled the bridle's headstall over the mare's ears, climbed on, and sitting straight and tall in the saddle like a cowboy, galloped her around the apple orchard in front of our house. It seemed I'd graduated, and he'd bought a horse who would go faster than a walk.

He rode the mare back to us and stepped off. "She'll do. She's gentle and sound and ought to be a good horse." He furrowed his brow and squinted at Veronica and me. "Now, just because she'll run doesn't mean you should be racing her around. I don't want you to get hurt. Be careful and take good care of her."

"What's her name?" I asked.

Daddy shrugged. "Don't know. She doesn't have registration papers, and I forgot to ask."

"Doesn't matter. I'd rather name her anyway." I stroked the mare's shiny neck and soft, black muzzle and gazed into the depths of her milk chocolate eyes. "She's so cute. Let's name her Babyface, like the song." It was a perfect name for her, but Babyface was more than cute. She was beautiful.

Veronica took the reins, and straightening the mare's forelock, nodded her agreement. Before my sister climbed on, Mama said, "Remember, it's you girls' job to take care of this horse, or she will be sold."

Giving Mama my most earnest look, I said, "Don't worry. I'll remember."

Veronica, though not horse-crazy like me, was athletic and a natural cowgirl. She made riding horseback look easy and had even made Billy trot.

She climbed on Babyface, then walked and loped the mare, zigzagging between apple trees. I could hardly stand the endless wait for my turn. After my sister had taken way too many trips around the orchard, she finally returned. My fingers entwined in the mare's mane, and Daddy boosted me on.

As I rode up our long dirt driveway, Babyface's rhythmic walk swayed me from side to side in a slow dance. With our matching blonde hair, I imagined how great we looked together, cowgirl and palomino. My elation ended abruptly when the thick grass growing along the driveway's edge tempted her. She thrust her head down, jerked the reins out of my hand, and began grazing.

I scrabbled to grab my lost reins, and we had a tug-of-war. Finally, she raised her head. We continued down the driveway and reached the county road. There I turned her back toward the house and kicked. When she broke into a butt-spanking trot, keeping my balance wasn't easy. I clutched the saddle horn and bounced up and down. Then, she started to lope. I couldn't stop laughing. I was flying.

After I rode up and down the driveway about twenty times, Daddy insisted I get off. He helped me unsaddle, and then clasping Babyface's lead rope, I led her up the hill and through the gate. After turning her loose, I saw she wasn't our only new horse. A round-bellied mare with a buckskin coat and black mane shimmering in the sun grazed in the pasture. Startled, her head came up when I approached and offered my open palm for her to smell. Her jet-black nostrils sniffed, and then sneezed, and then unconcerned, she returned to grazing.

I wiped my snot-wet hand on my jeans and then rushed down to the house and into the kitchen. "Mama, there's another horse in the pasture," I said while trying to catch my breath.

She ran her fingers through her short-cropped hair and frowned. "Oh yes, as usual, your daddy has gone overboard. He couldn't buy only one horse. She's a registered Quarter Horse. Her name is Snafu." Mama rinsed her hands in the kitchen sink and gazed out the window. "As if two horses weren't problem enough, soon we'll have three. She's going to have a foal."

"A foal," I said, my voice trembling with excitement. "When is she going to have it?"

Mama turned and gave me a hard stare. "I'm not sure, but soon. Those horses better not cause any problem. I don't need another worry."

"The horses won't be any trouble. I promise." Crossing my heart, I held up my right hand, determined to take care of the horses and not give

Mama any reason to be unhappy or upset and have one of her "headaches."

Chapter Four
Friends

Black-and-white spotted dairy cows grazed next door to our farm in a pasture surrounded by an electrified fence. I put my finger on the wire, and a pulse of electricity zinged up my arm. It almost shocked the pee out of me. I wouldn't be stupid enough to touch it again.

On the other side, an empty white farmhouse shared our driveway. In the field in front of it, rows and rows of green beans were planted all the way to the road. Before I could tromp between the muddy rows, a freckled-faced teenage girl crossed the road. She wore skintight jeans, and her blouse gapped where the buttons strained against her Maidenform bra. I bet she wore falsies.

"Hey, I'm Jenny Lee." She tipped her head in the direction of a green house across the road. "I'm visiting my grandma for the summer."

I gawked. With bright red lipstick smeared on her pouty lips and hair bleached like Marilyn Monroe's, she looked older than I was and city tough, like the kids in the movie *Blackboard Jungle*.

"I'm Winna. I just moved here." I pointed toward our house.

Squinting, she peered at it, then turned and brazenly stared at me. "So, what's to do around here, huh?"

Her eyes drilled into mine, and her intimidating gaze made me nervous. I shrugged and said, "I'm going to hike through this bean field."

I felt her staring at my back as she followed me into the forest of vines strung on beanpoles high above our heads. While we strolled through the string beans, black mud squished between my bare toes, and Jenny Lee's strong rose-scented perfume mingled with the musky odor of vegetation and damp earth.

Halfway down the row, Jenny Lee swatted at a ladybug crawling on a sticky leaf and said, "Don't ya hate school?"

Before she could squash it, I encouraged the ladybug to crawl on my finger. After admiring its shiny red-and-black-spotted shell, I held the tiny bug high and blew on it until it flew away. Then turning to Jenny Lee, I said, "I'm starting high school. Not sure I'll like it. What grade are you in?"

She wrinkled her brow as if trying to think. "Not sure. I'd be a senior, except they expelled me 'cause I ditched and missed so much school."

"So, you've quit?"

"They probably won't let me back in. Spent time in juvie after a stupid neighbor blamed me for stealing. You wouldn't believe what goes on in that place. What a bunch of jerks." She stretched her hand out for me to view her knuckles covered with blue dots and crosses. "Did these in juvie. Each tattoo means somethin'."

I didn't ask what. The tattoos weren't artistic, just ugly ink dots, not worth the risk of blood poisoning.

"I hate where I live," Jenny Lee said, wiping her hands on her jeans. "My no good Dad left. Me and my mom live in a ratty place. Wish I could live all the time with Grandma. Then maybe I could get a horse."

I nodded. "I love horses. Daddy bought us one."

"Yeah, saw ya riding. Can I ride it?"

"Maybe."

Too weird and too friendly, Jenny Lee told way-too-much-awful stuff about herself, things no one with good sense would tell. It was best to keep bad things about your family to yourself.

Even though I wanted to brag, I kept my mouth shut about Babyface and Snafu and kept hunting for beans. Strolling farther down the row, I squatted and riffled through the leaves for ripe beans hidden in the thick growth. I found a ripe pod and crunched into the crispy-green skin. The raw bean tasted kind of sweet, nothing like cooked beans.

"What are you guys doing?"

Busily searching through the leafy vines, I was startled by the voice behind me. I looked around, and a slender girl about my age stood above me. I rose from my knees and faced her, and she was a few inches taller than I was. Her cheeks dimpled, and braces tormented her mouth when she smiled. Her sky-blue eyes slanted up like a Siamese cat's, and her silver-blonde hair was pulled back in a long ponytail.

She was pretty. If it weren't for those braces, she'd be perfect. Me, I'd never be mistaken for pretty. With my round face, too-wide nose, and eyes set too close together, I'd be lucky to be considered cute.

"Picking green beans," I said. "They're good raw."

"I'm Trudy. Saw you riding your horse yesterday."

"You did?" I said, surprised. It seemed as if everyone in the neighborhood had seen me.

"I live up there." She pointed at a house on a hill. "I can see everything from my front window."

Jenny Lee narrowed her eyes and stared up at Trudy's house.

"I'm Winna." I raised my chin to look taller and offered Trudy a bean. She nibbled on the crunchy pod as we both looked at Jenny Lee, who said nothing, just kept gazing up at Trudy's.

I tipped my head toward her. "She's Jenny Lee and lives across the street."

"Want to see my new house?" Trudy asked. "I've got a brand-new canopy bed."

"Sure." I shrugged and pretended not to be too interested but could hardly wait to snoop inside. Ever since I'd spied it on the hill, I'd wondered who lived in such a big, fancy place. Jenny Lee better keep her trap shut about being in juvie. Trudy might not be so eager for us to see inside if she knew Jenny Lee was a thief.

We hiked up a steep dirt driveway to a yellow stucco house with a patio in the front yard, shaded by an ancient oak tree. I wiped my now dry, mud-crusted feet on the mat before going inside. Trudy swung open a door just inside the front entry and proudly displayed a lavender room with a shiny hardwood floor and white princess style furniture trimmed in gold.

"This is my room. Isn't it beautiful? Mom bought the canopy bed especially for my new bedroom and is making me a matching bedspread and canopy cover."

Until today, I'd never seen or even heard of a canopy bed, but I smiled and nodded, pretending I knew all about them. "Uh, very cool. My sister is thinking about getting one too."

Jenny Lee gazed mutely at the shiny, white dresser, probably eyeing the jewelry box on top and planning a heist. My hand slid over the smooth surface of Trudy's nightstand. This was definitely princess furniture. Her bedspread would probably be rose pink. Military drab and a twin bed was Mama's idea for my bedroom décor. She bought a brown army blanket from the Army-Navy Surplus Store for my bedspread because wool lasts forever and would keep me warmer than a "bear in a rug."

"You're lucky. I wish I had a sister." Trudy sighed, sat on her bed, and flipped back a wisp of blonde hair that had escaped her ponytail.

This was the first time having a sister was a plus. It wasn't a complete lie when I said, "Having an older sister *is* fantastic."

Trudy absentmindedly nodded and began chewing the tip of her ponytail. "I do have an older brother, though. He's starting college this fall."

"My sister is planning on going to college too," I said.

This really wasn't a lie, either. Last year, a somewhat homely but muscular neighbor boy broke Veronica's heart. In anguish over her lost love, she harped about men not being women's masters. She decided to be an independent woman and go to beauty college, become a model or airline stewardess.

"I'm a feminist and believe in free love," Veronica declared.

Not sure what the heck she meant, I said, "What's to believe. Isn't love supposed to be free?"

Tilting her chin, she huffed an impatient sigh and finger combed her hair. "You're so unsophisticated. You know nothing about male and female relationships. Marriage is a trap. I'm not having a bunch of kids to tie me down. I'm going to have a career and see the world."

I knew better than to ask any more questions when she gave me a you're-too-dumb-to-understand glare. She was right. Boys didn't interest me, and I'd never experienced love, not even the puppy variety. Love and sex were mysterious.

Once, while snooping through Veronica's room, I found the novel *Peyton Place* stashed under her mattress. I'd heard it was racy. Hoping it contained a bonanza of carnal knowledge, I riffled through pages hoping to find the shocking parts.

Mama caught me thumbing through it and snatched it out of my hand. "Ladies don't read books like this," she said and demanded to know where I'd gotten it.

Blushing with shame, I looked at the floor. "It's Veronica's."

Before I could learn more about sex other than what was whispered about or written on bathroom walls, Mama stomped outside and threw the book in the garbage can. When my sister found out, she rummaged through the trash to retrieve it. Man was she mad at me.

My attention returned to Jenny Lee when she cleared her throat and said, "College? I hate school."

Before she could blab about her depressing life as a juvenile delinquent and tell how she got kicked out of school, I quickly said, "This fall, I'm starting ninth grade. It'll be a while yet before I go to college."

"Me too," Trudy said. "Isn't it great? I move here from L.A. and right away make a friend who's in my grade and likes horses too. Can't believe my luck."

Making friends may be easier than I thought. To clinch the friendship, I said, "Come over sometime and ride Babyface."

Trudy's braces threatened to snag her lips when she smiled. "Oh, I'd love to. Soon I'll have my very own horse. Since we live in the country now, Mom promised to buy me one."

"I want to ride, too," Jenny Lee said.

Stupid me, I shouldn't have invited Trudy in front of Jenny Lee. Now I had to ask her. I nodded and said, "Yeah, sure."

We toured the rest of Trudy's home. From her living room window, she could see my house, the orchard and bean field in front, and even our barn roof. No wonder she saw me riding yesterday. So much for country privacy. Good thing lots of oaks surrounded the barnyard, or she'd be able to spy on everything I did from her princess perch.

"Thank you for the house tour," I said in my most ladylike tone of voice. We said goodbye, and then Jenny Lee and I strolled back down the hill to the bean field.

"What a beautiful house," Jenny Lee said. "Everything Trudy has is perfect. My drunken mom and I live in an ugly trailer. I hate it."

"Yep, Trudy sure has it made," I said.

Poor Jenny Lee. Her family was a mess. With her crazy life, it probably wouldn't matter to her my family was a mess too, but I didn't mention a thing about Mama. I couldn't talk about my problems the way she did. If people found out, nice girls with a nice family like Trudy's wouldn't want me for a friend.

Chapter Five
Going to Church

Sunday morning, Veronica and I dressed to go to church with Mrs. Barr. Wanting to look at least halfway decent, I burrowed through a tangle of coat hangers in my cramped wardrobe closet to find one of last year's school dresses that still fit. Choosing a green shirtwaist, I unbuttoned it, slipped it over my head, and stuck my arms through the sleeves. The hemline was shorter than the last time I wore it, and the bodice snugger against my barely emerging chest. I gazed in the mirror, from the front and then sideways. I didn't look the least bit sexy.

Going to church, wearing ladylike clothes, and worrying about how my hair looked weren't as much fun as wearing jeans, going barefoot, and riding horses. If I could, I'd vote against becoming a young lady the way Mama said. Of course, like most things, I didn't have a choice, but even if Mama didn't like it, I *could* have an opinion.

Veronica must have tried on everything in her closet. All of her rejects were scattered on the floor around her room. With her long legs, she looked great in all the latest fashions. She liked to tease me, saying my legs were so short they barely reached the ground. So unfunny.

Veronica fancied she would become a model after finishing high school, make tons of money, and travel all over the world. She was as pretty as the models in *Seventeen Magazine* and knew it. If they had high school classes on how to style your hair, do makeup, or admire yourself in the mirror for hours, with her flair for self-adornment, she'd get an A in everything. If she does go to college, her major will probably be glamour and boy chasing.

Me? I never imagined I'd be a model. When we shopped for school clothes, the latest styles looked lousy on me. I hated trying them on and looking at my reflection in the dressing room mirror was depressing. Tight skirts were either too tight or too loose. Big collars dwarfed me and made me look clownish, and Peter Pan collars looked priggish.

It was tiresome shopping for clothes and ending up buying the same dopey, old-fashioned shirtwaist dresses to hide my stocky thighs. Really, they were fat, but Mama insisted ladies never said people were fat, just plump or stout. Flat-chested, short-waisted, and not curvy in the right places, I dreaded when I'd have to undress for high school gym class in front of all the other girls. It was going to be so embarrassing.

When I started high school, I'd have to decide what classes to take and what to do with my life. Singing and drawing were fun, but I wasn't good enough to be a professional singer or artist. I hated the idea of being a nurse. Poking a needle in someone's arm gave me the willies. So that was out. I could learn to type and be a secretary, but that seemed boring. Training circus horses would be the most interesting and exciting job, more exciting than being a model. Plus, horses didn't care if you were pretty.

I combed my bobbed hair in the cramped bathroom and then returned to my room to slip on my too-tight Sunday shoes. Veronica finally dressed, emerged from her bedroom with an orange sweater draped over her shoulders like a queen's cape.

"Hurry up," Mama yelled from the kitchen. "Quit fussing over your clothes. It's almost 10:30. Mrs. Barr will be here any minute."

"I'm ready," Veronica said, patting her perfectly coiffed hair. "Why do we have to go to church, anyway? Already know what they're going to say. 'You're going to hell if you don't be good.' I've heard it before. How many times?"

"It won't hurt you to hear it again," Mama said. "We need to be reminded of the rules we should live by."

Veronica smirked and looked at me.

I rolled my eyes. Rules? Mama should go. She needed to be reminded too.

"After church, Mrs. Barr will be busy," Mama said. "I need to fill a prescription, so I'll pick you up at the drugstore."

When a car drove up, Mama combed her fingers through her hair and tightened the sash of her frayed, yellow robe. "She's here. Be nice." She opened the front door as Mrs. Barr stepped onto our porch, wearing a blue suit, a starched white blouse, and the same kind of sensible shoes she'd worn when I visited, except these looked new.

"Good morning," she said.

"How are you?" Veronica said in her sweetest voice. "It's so nice of you to take us to church. I've been so looking forward to it."

Veronica could be such a phony. We scooted out the door, past Mama, and Veronica jumped in the front seat. I sat behind Mrs. Barr in the back seat, and the odor of Blue Waltz Perfume permeated the old black sedan. Her pink scalp peeked through a coil of stringy hair knotted at the nape of her neck like a big wad of gray thread. How long did it take her to comb her few meager strands into a bun every morning, trying to make her hair look thicker?

We got to Arroyo Viejo, and as its name said, the town was old. Some of the stores with white-painted wooden facades could be in a cowboy movie. The date 1902 hung over the huge front door of a two-story red brick building. A three-story high building stood next to it. Built with large yellow stones, the numbers above its door gave the date it had been built,

1932. Telephone poles laced with thick electric lines, standing like sentinels guarding the main street, ended at a stone wall that protected a grassy graveyard from the shifting sand of the dunes.

Next to the graveyard, a church's white steeple loomed high, competing with the steeple of an identical looking church next door. Mrs. Barr parked her car behind them, in a graveled parking lot shared by both churches. We got out, walked to the front, and saw Jenny Lee and her grandmother going inside. Mrs. Barr left us and entered a small side door to join the choir, and Veronica led the way up cement steps and through tall double doors.

The church reeked of the lemony wood polish used to shine the dark wooden pews. A large wooden cross hung behind the pulpit, and the white-painted walls reflected bright sunlight radiating from rows of tall windows on opposite sides of the large room.

We sat in the last pew, and Veronica commented on everyone as they passed. "Look how enormous that old lady is. With her big rear-end, she'll need two seats."

A thin woman sat in the pew in front of us and draped an ugly fur over the back of the seat. Veronica looked at me, raised her eyebrows, and crossed her eyes. Then she whispered, "Why would anyone wear such an ugly green hat, or an awful fox fur, with paws, teeth and everything? Look, its beady eyes are staring at us."

Biting my lip to keep from giggling, I slinked down into my seat, afraid the woman overheard Veronica. The fox fur was truly terrible, with its shiny black, creepy toenails. Suppressing a giggle made me snort. Embarrassed, I covered my face and slid even farther down in the pew.

Mrs. Barr came in with the choir and sat behind the pulpit. Veronica kicked me, and I straightened up in my seat. Even though the hymn's page numbers were written on a board behind the choir for everyone to see, the choir director announced the first one. Then she raised her arms like the leader of an orchestra. The congregation stood to sing, and Veronica gave me the evil eye when I tried to hit the high notes of "The Old Rugged Cross."

After singing, the preacher stood at the pulpit. "Hell is waiting for those who do not follow the Lord," he preached. "Our neighbors next door aren't following God's word. No, they worship idols over there, right next door." He raised his hand, pointing his finger toward the neighboring church. "It's against the commandment that prohibits graven images. They have images, idols, a sin in the eyes of God. Satan likes to confuse us. Don't be fooled. Learn God's word and keep His commandments, every one of them, so that you will be saved."

The preacher blabbed on. Wearing a black robe like a judge, he waved his hands around like Moses parting the Red Sea and warned us about idols, sin, and burning in hell.

I was curious about the church next door. What did idols look like? I'd never seen one. They sounded scary, dangerous, interesting.

After more singing, it was time for the collection. Before Mama sent us off to church, she gave each of us money for the offering. "I'm keeping mine," Veronica whispered. "Let's get ice cream at the drugstore after church. Mama won't know if you don't tell."

I loved ice cream, and Veronica knew it. When the collection plate passed to me, my face warmed as I looked at all the dollars, lots of them. Guilt made my hand sweat as I clutched my money, feeling God's watching eyes and everyone else's.

Remembering the sweet taste of vanilla got rid of the bad feeling, and temptation got the better of me. After all, my few cents wouldn't matter to such a big collection. I pretended to drop in my coins, quickly passed the plate to Veronica, and glanced sideways to see her fake dropping coins into it too.

When the service was over, I walked outside and saw Jenny Lee standing with an older woman, probably her grandmother. I gazed over at the church next door and couldn't believe it. Trudy stood in front of the sinner's church, wearing a bright purple sweater and patent leather pumps. Did she go to the church the preacher said was wicked? I slipped through the shrubbery separating the two churches. She turned when I tapped her on the shoulder and said, "Hi, Trudy. Do you go to this church?"

Her hair was combed into a French twist, making her look older and more sophisticated than fourteen. "Oh, Winna. I didn't see you in church. Yes, we attend every Sunday, unless Mom has to work. Do you?"

"I was at the church next door. It's my first time. Our neighbor Mrs. Barr sings in the choir and invited us to go with her." I marched to the front door of her church. "The preacher said there are idols inside. Can I see them?"

As we entered her church, she said a bit huffily, "They're not idols. They're only statues."

Inside, colored light streamed through stained glass windows. The likeness of crucified Jesus hung on a gigantic cross behind the altar. A statue of the Virgin Mary, holding baby Jesus in her arms, stood off to the right. With a gentle, kind face, her life-like eyes gazed softly down. I liked these idols. It was peaceful in the sinner's church.

I lingered in front of the Virgin Mary's statue. "She's lovely," I said. "Do you think Mary actually looked like that?"

"Yes, I do. The statue of the Blessed Virgin and baby Jesus is my favorite. Mary's so beautiful. She cared for and nurtured Jesus when he was a helpless baby. She's the perfect Mother who belongs to us all." With her eyes transfixed on the ceiling, Trudy smiled. "She's up there now. Watching over us."

I looked up but saw nothing. What would a perfect mother be like? Was Jesus perfect because his mother was? If I needed a perfect mother to be a saint, I'd never make it.

Would Trudy go to hell because she went to the sinner's church? The idols seemed okay. The preacher must be wrong. God wouldn't condemn someone nice because there were a few statues in their church. It didn't make sense.

Anyway, I didn't care if she was a sinner and belonged to the wrong church. She wanted to be my friend, and making at least one true friend was on my list of goals and aspirations. Besides, except for Jenny Lee, there weren't any other girls in our neighborhood.

I nudged Trudy. "Do you want to get ice cream at the drugstore? Mama's picking us up there. You can ride home with us."

Trudy lowered her eyes. "I'll ask," she said, then hurried outside.

I followed her to the front of the church where her mom talked with people and then waited while she asked her.

Trudy got permission, and as we strolled toward the drugstore, my toes screamed inside my too-tight shoes. The town was small, but the stores had everything you'd need. Along the way, we passed a grocery store, a bakery with mounds of cream puffs in the window, and a movie theater.

Veronica must have invited Jenny Lee too. Just inside the drugstore's front door, they sat cross-legged on the floor by the magazine rack, eating ice cream, flipping pages, and looking at the latest teen fashions. Trudy and I bought cones, sat next to them to read comic books, and waited for Mama.

Before I finished licking my vanilla cone down to nothing, she showed up. Luckily, she didn't ask where we got the money to buy ice cream. She bought her prescription, and on the drive home, Trudy and I sat in the front seat. Veronica and Jenny Lee sat in the back, heads together, giggling and flipping pages of a magazine.

When we got home, I kicked off my shoes and went into Veronica's bedroom. She sat daintily on her bed, still thumbing through the fashion magazine. I knew she didn't have enough money to buy it, so I asked, "Did Jenny Lee buy that?"

Veronica gave me a defiant look. "She took it."

"Gads. You mean she stole it?"

"I guess you could say that."

"She stole it for you?"

"I guess."

"What if she got caught? You'd get in a lot of trouble."

Veronica smiled, and her eyes took on a cagey gleam like they did when she schemed. "No. Jenny Lee would be in a lot of trouble."

"You shouldn't have let her give it to you. It's like you stole it." I shook my head. "It's wrong. The drugstore man was nice to us."

Her smile dropped to a frown, and her eyes narrowed into slits. "You think you're so perfect? You stole from the church, didn't you?" She chopped the air with her fist and pounded the mattress like a gavel. "Didn't you?"

"What do you mean?"

She folded her arms across her chest. "This morning, when you didn't put the money Mama gave you into the church's offering, wasn't that stealing? Are you going to tell me you aren't guilty of stealing from the church? You did, didn't you?"

I stared at my rubbed-raw toes and said, "It didn't belong to the church because I never put it in the plate. Besides, it was your idea to get ice cream." Veronica was such a troublemaker, always trying to make me feel bad for doing stuff she'd thought up. Usually, she'd blame me and get me in trouble with Mama. This was way worse. Now she blamed me, saying I was the worst of sinners for stealing from God. She made me so mad I wanted to cry.

Chapter Six
Fifty-seven Chevy

The minute Veronica got her driver's license, she begged Daddy to let her buy a car. She said she wanted to play tennis and go out for cheerleading. With an extra car in the family, they wouldn't be bothered with driving her to after-school activities. He said no. Said he didn't want her to drive the kind of run-down piece of junk she could afford with the money she'd saved. This started her harping about Mama needing a car.

Finally worn down, Daddy agreed to buy a second car for Mama. He swore a Buick was the best car on the road, solid as a tank, but Veronica talked him into a Chevy because it was cool. Everyone said so. She secretly believed the car would actually be hers.

I had to stay home while everyone else went to town to buy the new car. After waiting around the house in anticipation, I heard a car in our driveway. I looked outside as our family's first Chevrolet rolled to a stop in front of the double garage door.

Wearing a huge grin, Veronica sat in the driver's seat of a two-tone, blue-and-white fifty-seven Chevy. I raced outside. My parents climbed out, and I jumped into the front seat that was also upholstered blue-and-white and wide enough for three people. I inhaled the heavenly new car fragrance and pleaded, "Can Veronica take me for a drive? Can she? Please."

Daddy had already gone into the house. Mama fiddled in her purse for a new pack of cigarettes. The cellophane crackled as she opened it and pulled out a cigarette. It seemed it took her forever to find a match to light it. Taking a huge drag, she squinted at us and nodded, then warned, "Be careful and drive slowly."

The Chevy practically crept down the driveway and onto the main road, but the second we were out of sight of our house, Veronica accelerated. My hair blew into tangles when I rolled down the window, poked my head out, and whooped. The breeze blew into my laughing mouth, and wind dried my tongue.

"You're acting like Puppy, hanging your head out of the window," Veronica squawked. "Shut your mouth. You'll be sorry if a bee flies in. Get your head inside the car. What a hick you are." The car veered when she took a hand off the steering wheel to slap my arm. Quickly grasping the wheel again, she stared intently out the windshield. "You better stop acting like an idiot, or I won't take you with me anymore."

I hadn't thought about bee stings. Closing my mouth, I pulled my head back in but kept the window open to let the breeze scour my face. Veronica slowed the Chevy when she saw Arroyo Viejo's city limits sign. Checking the rearview mirror, she said, "Mama would be hopping mad if I got a ticket."

Only a few cars were parked along the street, and no police cars in the City Hall parking lot. I sat straighter and finger-combed my hair as we drove the town's four blocks and passed the churches at the edge of the beach. The Chevy bounced over railroad tracks and onto an unpaved road through the dunes. We parked in the beach's unpaved parking lot and got out, and then Veronica locked the car.

A boardwalk separated the parking lot from the beach where greasy sunbathers lay on towels in the hot sand. Beyond the foamy white surf stretched an endless ocean, vast and desolate, flat as the desert on the other side of the wide canal behind our house on the cotton farm. Here it was cool, and the sun reflected off the ocean, sparkling and dancing over the water, instead of making wavy mirages the way it did when shimmering off the desert's broiling sand.

Along the boardwalk, a cart sold bright red, blue, and green Sno Kones. My mouth watered with anticipation of the sugary ice, but I didn't have any money.

I looked in the trash for soda bottles to redeem to get enough to buy a cone. A foul smell wafted from the can filled with half-eaten hotdogs and rotten, disgusting, no-telling-what-kind of garbage. Knowing I wanted a Sno Kone, Veronica tapped her foot and waited while I searched around for something to use to browse through the trash. I couldn't find anything, shrugged, and squelched my sweet desires.

Veronica stood in front of me and pointed her finger at my chest when I turned to keep walking down the boardwalk. "Missy sissy-wissy, are you afraid of a few germs like you're afraid of a few spiders?"

Tempted to spit in her face like an angry cat, I thrust back my shoulders, raised my chin, and glared. "And you're not? Why don't you use your bare fingers to dig in the garbage?" I wrinkled up my nose. "It stinks, but if a bottle were in all that mess, I wouldn't be afraid to pick it out. One bottle wouldn't buy anything anyway. Sno Kones cost more than a few cents."

Farther down the beach, teenage boys yelled and kicked sand while playing a game of volleyball. A dark-haired hunk of a boy stood a head taller than the others. Wanting to be noticed, Veronica walked ahead. Sashaying her hips, she pretended we weren't together and ignored me the way she usually did when she was with her friends.

She worked so hard trying to look cool it was disgusting. Was it cool if you had to try to be, or say the word "cool" because everyone else did? Trying to be cool was really un-cool. Mama said when Veronica's breasts grew, her brain shrank, and she turned boy crazy. That wasn't going to happen to me. I only had room in my heart to be crazy about horses, not boys.

Ignoring her ignoring me, I strolled to the edge of the blue-gray ocean's churning surf. The salty sea breeze was *cool*, and foamy waves broke close to the shore, rushing back and forth. Gulls flew overhead, occasionally swooping down to catch a fish or snack on the remains of a discarded lunch. Clumps of stinky seaweed dotted the shoreline, with chunks of rotting pink crabs entangled in its brown leathery leaves and hose-like vines.

My bare feet left prints in the hard, damp sand. Nearby, hoofprints had dug up the sand, and up the shore about a mile away, horseback riders galloped in the sudsy surf. Wow! I could ride Babyface on the beach.

I had no bathing suit but couldn't resist wading into the ocean. I misjudged the depth of the water and the power and size of the unpredictable waves. A big one came in and tumbled me under. The churning water held me down. Desperately needing a gulp of air, I was sure I would drown until the wave washed me up on shore, where it was shallow enough to stand.

Veronica rushed into the surf to help me struggle to my wobbly feet. Together we stumbled out of the surf to the dry beach and plopped down. She took on a bossy, big-sisterly tone. "What were you doing out there? You could have drowned."

Feeling like a wet rag doll, I wiped the salty snot running from my nose with the back of my hand and blinked my burning eyes. Still gasping for a breath, I sputtered, "Don't tell Mama. I'm okay, except my nose and eyes sting awful."

Veronica wagged a warning finger in my face, but then she nodded.

Waiting for the sun to dry my sopping wet hair, shirt, and shorts, we sat in the sand and watched people stroll by. Sand clung to my damp skin and crept inside my shorts, making my undies grate on my skin like sandpaper.

The boys playing volleyball didn't look our way, and Veronica, so used to boys falling all over her, became bored. "Come on," she said. "Let's go."

Before we got into the car, she noticed my still damp and sandy clothes. "You're going to get sand inside our new car. Go to the bathroom and use some paper towels to dry off."

In one of the toilet stalls, I stripped down, used tons of paper towels, then shook as much sand from my clothes as I could and got dressed. When I got back to where the Chevy was parked, Veronica stood with hands planted on her hips and the corners of her mouth upside-down.

"Come on, hurry up," she said. "Sit in the back. Maybe Mama won't notice any sand there."

Veronica watched while I spread paper towels on the back seat and climbed in without an argument. In the driver's seat, she gripped the steering wheel, then turned and glared at me before carefully backing out of the parking space. "We get a new car, and right away, you mess it up. I can't wait to graduate. Then no more tag-alongs."

With her angry face reflecting in the rearview mirror, she drove and complained. "I don't want to be like Mama, get married, do housework, and be stuck at home with a bunch of brats. I'm going to have a life. Things have changed. It's a big world, and I'm going to see it."

Was Mama unhappy because of us, I wondered? Did she wish she'd had a career instead of getting married and having kids? Maybe she was sorry she hadn't gone to college, but most girls didn't when she was young. It was 1957, and things *were* different now, and women could do more stuff, even become a horse trainer. Did I want to go to college? Right now, I just hoped to survive ninth grade.

On the drive home, the breeze blowing through the open window dried my hair. It was sticky with salt and felt awful. My shirt was stiff, and I hadn't gotten all the sand out of my shorts. It still grated inside my underwear.

Veronica parked the car in the garage and told me to get the vacuum. Luckily, Mama and Daddy must have been in their room when I went into the house, so no questions about what I was going to do with it.

I sucked up the sand I'd shed on the back seat and then put the vacuum away. When I came back outside, Trudy and Jenny Lee stood watching while Veronica busily polished the Chevy with one of Daddy's old T-shirts.

"Wow, what a great car," Jenny Lee said. Her red sweater and pegged jeans couldn't have been tighter. She smiled, and a glob of red lipstick clung to a front tooth.

"Yes, it's beautiful." Veronica nodded and kept polishing the Chevy's hood.

Trudy's finger trailed along the Chevy's side. "My brother's car isn't half this nice."

Veronica stopped wiping and turned. "You have an older brother?"

"Yes. His car is a real jalopy. He works on it all the time to keep it running."

Veronica tilted her head, and with a Mona Lisa mysterious smile, turned back to polishing the car.

"Daddy bought the car for Mama," I said. "But we drove it to the beach. It was great. People rode horseback in the surf. Wouldn't it be fun? I'd rather ride a horse than drive a car."

"Me too," Trudy agreed but kept admiring the Chevy's shiny paint.

"Let's go up to the barn," I said. "Maybe Snafu had her foal. I can hardly wait to see the new baby."

Jenny Lee offered to help Veronica polish the car, and Trudy and I raced up the hill trail. In the pasture, Babyface and Snafu grazed side by side. "I read mares get milk the day before they foal." I peered under Snafu's belly for any change in her udder. "I don't see anything yet. Let's give 'em some hay."

We stepped out of the bright sun, and our eyes adjusted to the dim light of the musty smelling barn. Trudy had never been inside and said, "This old barn is so cool."

"Yeah, uh, cool. I bet they built it in the cowboy days."

Trudy gazed up at the old rough-hewn rafters. "My mother said Frank and Jesse James lived around here somewhere." Her eyes widened as she looked at me. "The dirt road behind your pasture is named Stagecoach Road."

"Wow? Bandits may have robbed stagecoaches like in the movies and hid the loot here. We should go on a treasure hunt."

"Buried treasure? Where?" Veronica asked as she and Jenny Lee entered the barn.

"Right here." I grinned and waved my hand around.

Veronica smirked and glanced at Jenny Lee. "Where would you start looking? This barn is so big you'd be digging forever. Treasure, what a dumb idea."

Trudy, Jenny Lee, and Veronica all got the giggles, about what I hadn't the faintest idea. As usual, when my sister showed up, she became the center of attention. Would she make it harder to be friends with Trudy? If the three of them buddied up, I'd become the tag-along little sister.

Chapter Seven
Riding Babyface

If I wanted to ride, I had to catch Babyface. Daddy usually did, but he went to the doctor's office to have a bunch of tests, and Veronica had gone over to Jenny Lee's. Babyface was tricky to catch, but if I was going to be a horse trainer, I had to figure out how.

The horses snoozed in the shade of an oak. When they heard me coming, they roused and quietly watched me stroll up. Catching Babyface looked as if it were going to be easy until I got next to her shoulder and tried to reach up to wrap the lead rope around her neck.

She raised her head, twirled, and took off at a dead run with Snafu right behind her. They raced toward the fence at the back edge of the pasture like two thoroughbreds in the Kentucky Derby. On the hilltop, they stopped, stood at attention, and waited, watching me hike toward them as I trudged down one steep hillside and up another.

By the time I finally got close enough again to catch Babyface, I huffed and puffed like the big, bad wolf. Under their scrutiny, I strolled up to her, but this time I hid the halter behind my back. I tried to sneakily reach up to put the lead rope around her neck, but before I could, she jerked away again, took off like a flash with Snafu on her heels, and galloped back to the oak tree where the chase first started.

Panting more than if I'd climbed the Matterhorn, my face and armpits were sticky with sweat by the time I hiked back to where the horses again napped under the tree. Babyface swished flies with her long white tail, calculating when it was time to race back to the other end of the pasture. At this rate, I'd never catch this wily mare, and I might die of exhaustion chasing her up and down the pasture hills.

When I helped Daddy, we'd corner the horses, and he never had trouble haltering them. With no help and without studying Professor Beery's course yet, how could I catch a horse who didn't want to get caught? I'd seen movies where a person used telepathy to read other people's minds and motives. How could I tune into my psychic abilities and read Babyface's mind?

I shut my eyes and tried to empty my brain of thoughts, but it wasn't easy. They kept popping into my head. I'd force one out, and another hopped in. Minutes passed with me pushing out thoughts, trying to contact the animal world psychically.

A giant-sized horse sneeze made me open my eyes. Babyface's large, chocolate brown eyes peered at me. Was she reading *my* mind? What was she thinking? Maybe I should pretend I didn't want to catch her. I meandered toward the barn, and when I looked back, surprise, surprise, the mares followed me. Gads, I was an idiot. I should've thought of this before.

Going inside the barn, I climbed to the top of the haystack and threw a flake of hay into the manger. The mares trotted inside and shoved their noses into the hay. After slowly closing the barn's huge door, I crept up to Babyface sing-songing softly, "Easy girl. How are you today? Nice girl."

When I stood at her shoulder, she raised her nose out of the manger. Holding my breath, I stretched out my flattened hand. She sniffed it, then noogied her lips on my empty palm, searching for a treat. Leaning against her warm neck, I closed my eyes and melded into her rhythmic breathing. Peaceful warmth washed over me.

Babyface broke my mood with a snort. I stroked her, stood on my tiptoes, wrapped my arms around her neck, and looped the lead rope around it. I buckled the halter on and tried to lead her, but she pulled against it, wanting to stay in the barn to eat with Snafu. I swatted her shoulder, and then she followed as I led her down to the garage where the saddle was kept.

After brushing her golden coat to a silky sheen, I faced another problem. She was so tall. How could I lift the saddle that high? In the garage, a wooden crate leaned against the wall. It looked about the right height to help me be tall enough. Babyface patiently watched as I lugged the box over to place it next to her. Stepping up on it, I put the thick saddle blanket on her back.

I went into the garage and dragged the heavy saddle to where Babyface waited. I climbed on the box again. The saddle weighed a ton when I tried to hoist it high enough to place it on her back. While I struggled with the saddle, the blanket slipped off and fell in the dirt.

Laying the saddle on the ground next to Babyface, I shook the dust off the blanket the best I could. I tried to heave the saddle back up again, and it became a war to keep the blanket in place. Frustrated, I was determined to win the battle. My arms were so tired they trembled when I finally managed to get the saddle on and cinched up.

Next problem, Babyface wouldn't lower her head to be bridled, and my idea of talking sweetly to her didn't work. What a witch! I moved the box, set it on the ground next to her head, and then stood on it. She clenched her teeth when I offered her the bit. Sliding my thumb into the corner of her mouth the way Daddy did, I wedged the bit between her teeth.

It worked. Babyface opened her mouth wide enough for me to shove in the bit. Standing on my tiptoes, I slipped the headstall over her stiff, fuzzy ears and then tidied her blonde forelock. I got off the box, straightened the tangled reins, and sighed. Being a horse trainer wasn't going to be easy.

Now, how would I get on? Veronica was an acrobat and could grab a handful of mane and swing on like a real cowgirl. Me, I had to stand on the box and get on ballerina style.

Pointing my toe, I kicked high enough to anchor my foot into the stirrup. Babyface calmly stood while I clutched the saddle strings and struggled to boost myself high enough to swing my leg over her back. Before I was even halfway up, she snorted and sighed a huge sigh.

The saddle began slipping. Frantically I clung to the saddle horn as slowly, slowly, inch-by-inch it slid sideways. It kept sliding until it was all the way under her belly. Hanging upside down for a moment like a spider monkey, I let go and dropped flat on my back in the dirt.

Babyface's hairy underside loomed above me. Acting innocent, she turned her head to gawk as I scooted out from under her and scrambled out of the dirt. Bent over with my hands on my knees, I tried to catch my breath. Straightening up, I slapped the dust off my pants and glanced around, hoping no one had seen Babyface make a fool out of me, especially Trudy, who was probably perched on her hill, watching.

Heck with it! I uncinched the upside-down saddle that dangled like a loose tooth under her belly. It dropped on the ground. Babyface slyly watched as I dragged the heavy saddle back to the garage. Something told me she had planned this.

"You think you've tricked me, don't you, girl? Well, you've won. I'm not putting the saddle on again." Leading her to the front porch, I climbed up on the top step and jumped on her bareback. "Okay, Babyface, let's go."

With nothing but her mane to clutch for security, I gathered the reins and zigzagged between the apple trees. As she walked, Babyface's back muscles rippled under me, and her salty sweat dampened my pant legs. I turned her out of the orchard and rode down the driveway.

When I reached the road and turned back toward my house, Trudy stood at the edge of the bean field. She waved. "Hey, hi. I saw you riding and came down."

Trudy walked beside Babyface and didn't say anything about seeing me dumped when I tried to saddle my horse. Back at my house, I maneuvered the mare next to the porch and said, "Jump on."

She struggled up behind me, clung to my waist, and we rode double to the pasture. Once we got through the gate, barn sour Babyface had her own idea where she wanted to go. Before I could stop her, the stubborn mare swiftly turned and sprinted toward the barn.

"Oomph!" I flopped in the dirt, and ton-of-bricks Trudy landed on top of me. A gallon of air swooshed out of my chest like a deflated balloon.

I wiggled out from under her. My gut hurt. I curled into a ball and took deep breaths to help untie the knot in my belly. It didn't work, so I turned over and stretched out on my back. Above me, clouds swirled like mares' tails in the sky. A few moments passed before I got to my feet.

Trudy still lay flat on her back. I spat the dirt out of my mouth and asked, "Are you all right?"

"I'm catching my breath. It was a long way down."

"That's for sure. Thought maybe you'd broken something, besides me." I offered my hand to help Trudy up.

Babyface dumping us wouldn't win me any friendship points. When we'd fallen off, she had stopped and turned to look down at us as if she enjoyed seeing us lying in the dirt and wanted to savor the moment. Irritated, I snatched up her reins and said, "You're wicked."

"Well, at least she waited for us," Trudy said, bending down to pick foxtails out of her socks.

We plucked wisps of dry grass and stickers out of each other's shirts and hair. Babyface watched us, probably secretly sniggering.

I wasn't hurt, but I felt quaky after hitting the ground so hard and was a little worried about climbing back on. Wanting to be a good horseback rider and learn to train horses more than anything, I remembered the time Daddy taught me to ride a two-wheeler, and I'd fallen and skinned my knees bloody. He'd said, "Get back on, or you'll never get your balance."

It was probably Trudy's fault I'd lost my balance and fallen off. Not wanting to be dumped off again and be her squashed-flat pillow, I said, "Let's take turns riding by ourselves."

"You first," Trudy said, combing her fingers through her ponytail, feeling for stickers.

To get on Babyface again, I needed something high to stand on. The water trough by the gate looked high enough, so I led her next to it. A bit queasy and hesitant to get back on, I took a deep breath, gulped down my uneasiness, and hopped on anyway.

I kicked her to ride back to the pasture and away from the barn. Before I could tightly clutch her mane, she broke into a trot, and with a quick turn, detoured toward the barn. My sweaty pant legs didn't keep me glued to her back. I slipped sideways and tumbled hard to the ground.

Out of breath, I wasn't hurt but was angry and humiliated. Babyface stood staring at me. I got up, grabbed the reins, marched her over to Trudy, and offered her the reins to take her turn. She shook her head and continued sitting in the shade.

At this rate, I'd never be a horse trainer. Too mad to give up, I needed to figure out how to keep Babyface from running to the barn. Before climbing back on her, I sat for a minute listening to bees buzz and considered. Hadn't she pinned her ears back just before she changed directions?

When I got on her this time, I entwined my fingers in her long mane, clamped my legs around her body, and then kicked her into a trot. As I scrutinized her golden ears, sure enough, they flattened before she twirled. Ready for her naughty behavior, I stayed on when she swerved into a sharp turn and ran toward the barn. I leaned down low on her neck and ducked as she raced under the huge door. Once inside, she stopped, turned her head and waited, expecting me to fall off.

Trudy rushed into the barn and said, "I thought you were a goner."

I tried to act like a cowgirl, even though my breath came in short gulps. "Naw, I figured out one of Babyface's tricks. All you do is watch her ears. When she pins 'em back, she's planning to take a quick zigzag back toward the barn. Then you hang on tight. Get on and try it."

Trudy didn't seem to buy my fake bravado. Even so, when I rode back to the trough and slid off, she squared her shoulders, took a few deep breaths, and then climbed on again. Except, she didn't make Babyface trot. Instead, she kept her at a walk and allowed the mare to stroll straight into the barn.

I followed them inside. Trudy looked at me and said, "I'm getting to be a good horseback rider." Babyface had been naughty, but Trudy patted and praised her for being such a good girl.

Though Trudy's over-inflated opinion of her riding skills was difficult to swallow, with a smile, like a lady, I did. I even kept my trap shut about her encouraging my horse's bad behavior.

She slid off the mare and held out the reins. "I'm hungry. Let's walk to my house. I'll make lunch."

"We can ride Babyface," I said.

"Do you think that's a good idea?"

"Oh, sure. Come on. I'll lead her down to the house. She'll act way better when she's not near the barn."

Hoping I was right, I led the mare down to my front porch and jumped on. Trudy stood on the porch and acted doubtful about getting on behind me.

"Watch," I said and trotted Babyface down our driveway. I reached the road, then turned and loped back to the porch. "See, she's good when she's away from the barn."

Trudy shrugged. "I hope so," she said and struggled up behind me.

Babyface acted nice as pie as we rode her up the hill and tethered her to the dead tree in Trudy's front yard. It was hard not to be impressed when we went into her fancy, sunshine-bright kitchen with a built-in dishwasher and oven and a shiny white fridge humming in one corner.

My stomach growled in protest while watching Trudy perform her sandwich-making ritual. Opening a can of tuna, she put it in a bowl, then slowly chopped sweet pickles into itty bits, and, with a gob of mayonnaise, stirred them into the tuna and meted out precisely equal portions on slices of toasted wheat bread. From the cupboard, she retrieved white dinner-sized plates and neatly placed the sandwiches on them.

Trudy set two plates on the table with blue paper napkins and filled tall red tumblers with orange soda. We sat at a dinette in front of a window overlooking the valley below. As hungry as a wolf, I wanted to gobble down the sandwich, but practiced my manners and said, "How lovely," and then took small ladylike bites, chewing thoroughly with my mouth closed.

While we ate, the back door leading in from the garage opened. A plump woman with light brown hair, wearing a nurse's uniform, came in. She smiled when she saw us.

Trudy swallowed her bite of sandwich and said, "Hi, Mom. This is Winna."

"Hello, Winna. That must be your horse tied outside."

"Her name is Babyface," Trudy said. "I've been riding her all over the pasture at Winna's. I'm getting to be good at equitation. All that exercise made us hungry, so I made lunch."

"Good thing you're becoming a good rider because this morning I called a man about a horse. He'll deliver it tomorrow. What do you think?" Her mom grinned and studied Trudy's face.

Trudy screamed, "A horse. Am I getting a horse? I can hardly wait. What color is it? Is it a mare? What time will it get here?" Her questions came so fast I could barely understand her.

"Your horse should arrive around noon," Trudy's mom said. "Before it does, you need to check the pasture fence."

Trudy retrieved a stepladder out of her garage to use to climb on Babyface. We rode to the pasture down the hill from her house and checked the fence for broken wires that could cut or entangle Trudy's new horse tomorrow.

*****

Around noon the next day, I hiked over to see if Trudy had gotten her horse. In her yard, she was brushing a black mare with two white socks on her hind legs and a white strip down the middle of her forehead.

When I walked up, she stopped brushing and turned, and a wired buck-toothy smile spread across her face. "Isn't she beautiful? Her nickname's Blackie, but her real name's Black Bow. She's half Morgan and half Quarter Horse." Flipping back her ponytail, she tilted her head and wiped her forehead with the back of her hand, leaving a streak of dirt. "Don't you just love her? This is the best gift ever." She wrapped her arms around Blackie's neck and squeezed.

Her mom came outside. Happy tears trickled down Trudy's cheeks as she transferred the hug to her mom's neck. "Thank you, Mom. I've wanted a horse forever. She's so beautiful."

"Remember, this gift comes with responsibilities. You must take care of her. Make sure she's fed and watered. She depends on you. Everyday. No one else but you, understand?" Trudy's mom looked at her, expecting a reply.

"Yes, yes. I'll be sure Blackie has hay every day and keep her water trough filled. I won't forget." Trudy returned to brushing the mare, polishing her silken coat. "It's so exciting. Now we can trail ride together."

"Let's go for a ride now," I said. "I'll go get Babyface."

Hurrying back to my house, I climbed the hill trail to the barn hoping the mare hadn't figured out my hay-in-the-barn-to-catch-her trick.

I stopped at the gate, surprise. A tiny, chocolate brown filly, with a perfect white blaze, stood at Snafu's side by the water trough. An ugly stump that once attached her belly button to her mama still dangled.

The new baby braced her long, wobbly legs and nudged Snafu. The mare grunted and licked her foal as the little one reached up and nose butted her mother's belly in search of milk. The filly found the udder and started to nurse.

I went through the gate, and when I stepped closer, the new mother's head came up. Snafu's ears flattened back, warning me away. Scared to get too close to her new foal, I said, "Easy, easy, Snafu. I know you're a good mother protecting your foal, but I won't hurt your baby."

Rushing down to the house to tell everyone, I entered the back door and yelled, "Snafu had her baby! It's a filly!"

As Daddy, Mama, Veronica, and I climbed the hill trail to the pasture to see the newborn, Veronica screamed, "Daddy!" and grabbed his elbow as he slipped and fell to his knees.

I dashed to help him up. "Daddy, are you all right!"

"I'm okay. I'm okay. Calm down. Just wasn't paying attention. Slipped on some loose dirt and lost my balance."

"You know the doctor said to be careful," Mama said as she dusted off his pants. "You need to take care of your bad foot. You shouldn't be climbing this hill. Let's go back to the house."

"No, I want to see Snafu's new filly." Daddy smiled. "Nothing cuter than a newborn foal. I'm fine. Don't worry." He insisted, and Veronica held his hand to steady him, and we continued up the trail.

The mares and foal still stood next to the gate, drinking from the trough. "Isn't she prettier than anything?" I said.

"Pretty is as pretty does. This foal is going to create more chaos," Mama said, but she couldn't keep from grinning.

Daddy nodded. "I'm sure this little girl will create some chaos around here."

Then his eyes twinkled, and he smiled. "It fits her pedigree, Chaos out of Snafu."

While everyone admired the filly, Snafu pinned her ears at us and nudged her foal away with her muzzle. "All right, then," Daddy said. "Let's leave the new mother and our little Chaos alone. Snafu's upset, trying to protect her new baby. After a few days, she'll quiet down. Until then, be careful. Walk and talk quietly around her. Don't get too close, or the mare might get mad."

Snafu flattened her ears to confirm what Daddy said. I knew he was right, but I could hardly wait to make friends with Chaos. Wait and be patient. I must be patient and win Snafu's trust before I could pet her foal. Then we'd become friends.

Before going through the gate, I gazed one more time at the beautiful new filly. Then I hurried to catch up with Veronica and Mama, who helped Daddy back down the steep path to the house.

Chapter Eight
New Kids

In the late afternoon of Chaos's birthday, a moving van bounced up the long driveway we shared with the farmhouse next-door and parked in the neighbor's yard. Soon after, an Oldsmobile sedan arrived pulling a horse trailer. A man, woman, tall teenage boy, and younger girl got out. The pigtailed girl hugged a Raggedy Ann doll against her chest and looked about ten-years-old.

The movers hustled out of their van and rushed around, unloading furniture. Doors opened and slammed shut. The mom yelled at the movers for banging their stuff around. The dad and boy unloaded a horse from the trailer and led it to the pasture behind the house. What a stroke of luck! A family with kids and a horse had moved right next door.

*****

Early the next morning, fresh coffee perked in the coffee pot, but our kitchen was empty. I heated milk, made a cup of cocoa, and plopped down at our yellow chrome dinette. With no one to correct my table manners, I propped my feet on a chair and, with elbows on the table, noisily sipped the hot cocoa. If Mama were here, she'd complain, "A lady doesn't sound like a slurping pig."

I finished my cocoa, and Puppy followed me when I wandered next door to spy on the new neighbors' house. Crouching behind their front yard hedge, I whispered, "Sit, Puppy," and then peeked through thick, woody brambles.

On the ground nearby, I heard, plunk, plunk.

High in a giant tree, the neighbor boy was picking and tossing down avocados. He stopped, and hanging onto a limb, leaned sideways, and yelled, "Hey, down there. What are you doing?"

How embarrassing! He caught me peeping like a nosey Tom. Not wanting to be bashed on the head with one of the green-black avocados, I stood and stepped from behind the bush. Tongue-tied and mind empty of a clever excuse, I pointed toward my house. "I, uh, live next door."

"Yeah, I know. Saw you walk over."

He swung down from the branch like an orangutan and strutted up to me. A head taller than I was, he had a perfect movie star nose, a dimpled square jaw, and funny cowlicks swirled in his sandy-brown crewcut hair. His T-shirt must have shrunk a size in the wash the way it fit so snugly across his broad shoulders.

Staring down at me with brown-flecked green eyes, he said in a deep voice, "I'm Ben."

My face turned warm under his scrutiny. My hair must have looked a mess. I hadn't combed it before I'd left the house. Blushing and gazing at my feet, I managed to stammer, "Uh, hi. I'm, uh, Winna."

Puppy wagged her tail.

"Nice dog," he said and scratched behind her ears. "With those two black ears, she looks like the RCA Victor dog."

He sauntered to his front porch, jerked open the screen door, and went into his house. I must have looked like a complete dope peering at him through the porch screen. He picked up something and came back outside with a large, brown bag and a little sack.

"You like sunflower seeds?" Ben tore open the sack. "Have some. No salt. I like 'em better that way."

After I took a few seeds, he poured himself a handful, tossed the black-and-white-striped seeds into his mouth, crunched, then spit, aiming and firing the broken shells at an imaginary target on the ground. He must have had a lot of practice because he did it perfectly, almost slobber-free.

Mama said ladies didn't spit, so even though I wanted to gobble a handful and have a seed-spitting contest, I ate one seed at a time, daintily plucking the shells from my mouth.

As we strolled back to the avocado tree, Ben said, "Dad manages my baseball team and always makes sure we have plenty of sunflower seeds."

"You play baseball?"

"Yeah, I'm a pitcher. Played with the All-Stars back home."

A hotshot baseball player would be popular. Guess that left me off his girls-to-be-friends-with list.

Under the tree, Puppy nosed an over-ripe avocado. Before she could wolf it down and make herself sick, I snatched it from her and then helped Ben sack avocados in the paper bag. Soon we'd found all the ones hidden under the dry, brown leaves, and Ben took the full bag to the porch.

When he came back outside, as if I didn't already know, I asked, "Do you have a horse?"

"Yeah, sure do."

"Me, too."

"Should exercise her today," Ben said. "Her muscles need a stretch after such a long ride in the horse trailer yesterday. Want to see her?"

I nodded, and he led me to his backyard. When he whistled, his horse galloped down the hill to the gate.

Wow! How could I get Babyface to do that?

Ben's horse was a mare with a long red mane and tail. "She's pretty," I said. "If you're going for a ride, wait for me, and I'll get my horse."

Not wanting to be left behind, I rushed up the hill trail to our barn and tried whistling like Ben, but my breathy tweet sounded pitiful, not anything like his earsplitting whistle. I gave up on the idea and tossed hay in the manger. With tiny Chaos scrunched against her side, Snafu gave me the evil eye when the horses entered the barn.

While the mares ate, I closed the barn door and then carefully approached Babyface, hiding the bridle behind my back. She kept an eye on me but let me catch and bridle her.

From the edge of the water trough, I jumped on bareback and then rode to Ben's front yard, where he brushed his horse's dark, rusty colored coat.

"What's your horse's name?" I asked.

"Sugar, 'cause she's sweet." Ben smiled and patted Sugar's neck. "She's a mustang. What's your horse's name?"

"Babyface, 'cause she's cute."

"My girlfriend rides a pinto," Ben said.

"You have a girlfriend?" I asked, not sure why Ben having a girlfriend perturbed me.

"Yeah. Back in Modesto, where I used to live. Now that we've moved, I'll probably never see her again."

"Oh, too bad," I said, even though I was glad.

Ben's biceps bulged when he slung a saddle on Sugar. After cinching it, instead of stepping into the stirrup, he grabbed the saddle horn and swung up on Sugar's back. Was this how he always got on or was he trying to impress me?

"Let's ride in Sugar's pasture," he said.

Going through the gate behind his house, we rode up a steep path surrounded by tall coyote bushes growing higher than our heads. At the top, the hill flattened along the fence line where our pastures bordered behind our old barn.

Snafu and Chaos heard us ride up and came out of the barn with heads held high. Seeing Babyface, Snafu whinnied a "hello" and trotted over, but made a dead stop and stared when she saw Sugar and Ben. Protective of her foal, she pinned her ears and herded Chaos away from the fence.

"The mare is named Snafu, and her new baby is Chaos. They're Quarter Horses."

Ben laughed. "Your horse is named Snafu? My dad uses that word all the time. He learned it in the army."

"Oh? It is a funny word," I said. "What does it mean?"

"It's an acronym for Situation Normal, All Fouled Up," Ben said, and then scrunched his brow. "My dad fought in Korea. He said everyone worried the Russians might start World War III, but in his opinion, we should instead worry about the Red Chinese because they were behind the Korean War."

I shook my head and said, "My dad wasn't in the army but knows all about training horses. He's going to help me train the filly." I didn't like to think about war. It scared me. At school, we did drills, hiding under our desks in case the Russians dropped an A-bomb.

Ben looked at me. "You're training the filly?"

"Yep." I grinned. "Would you like to help me? The way you trained Sugar to come when you whistled is really cool."

Ben puffed out his chest. "Yeah, sure. I know a lot about horses. I'd be glad to help."

Visions of Ben and me training Chaos reeled through my mind like a movie. Feeling a bit giddy, I said, "Got to get Chaos used to people first, though. Let's tie our horses, and you can see inside our barn. We better not get near Chaos yet. Snafu is acting mean protecting her new baby."

We tethered our horses to fence posts, and then Ben stepped on the strands of barbed wire to stretch them apart, wide enough for me to crawl through the fence. Squeezing between the wires, I snagged my shirt. He stepped close to unhook the nasty sharp barb, and an electric tingle shot through me, pleasant and exciting, not like the jolt I got from the neighbor's fence.

Once freed, I held the wires apart for him too. As he slipped through the opening, my fingers trembled, and my heart thumped faster like a character in one of my sister's dumb romance novels.

Gads, I hoped he hadn't noticed. I'd always thought Veronica acted so stupid about boys. Now here I was on the brink of being boy-silly, too.

"What a great old barn," Ben said when we stepped into its twilight. The old green tractor grabbed his attention, and he scrambled up on its rusty seat. "Old tractors are cool. This one looks like it hasn't been used in years. Will it start?"

"Don't know."

"It'd be great to get it running. Old engines are fun to work on." Ben climbed off the tractor and peered at it. "Pretty dirty. Looks like the rats and spiders have taken over."

Pretending I knew about cars, I said, "We just got a fifty-seven Chevy."

"Wow, that's a great car. My dad has a fifty-one Oldsmobile. I help him work on it. Keep it tuned up, change oil, and do other mechanical stuff." He wiped his dusty hands on his jeans. "I'm going to be a mechanic. Been taking shop classes at high school. Learning how to rebuild engines."

His green eyes lit up as he gazed at me. I gulped, fought the urge to wipe the dirt smudge off his nose, and asked, "What grade are you in?"

"I'll be a junior this year."

Oh, drat. Ben was in my sister's grade. Lowering my gaze, I toed loose straw and said nothing about being a freshman.

Next, the hangman's rope caught his attention. He climbed on the haystack, grabbed the thick swinging rope, then shimmied to the top, grasped the barn's center beam, and did three chin ups. Sliding back down to the bottom of the rope, he swung, soared back and forth, and yelled, "Aaah-eee-aaah."

"Watch out!" He leaped and landed next to me at the foot of the haystack.

Ben looked like a short-haired Tarzan, not at all like an orangutan. "You want to see another cool place?" I asked, all atwitter, sure he must have shown off just for me.

We walked to the edge of the steep hill overlooking the meadow, where I'd found a reddish flat rocky ledge pockmarked with bowl-like hollows. I'd dubbed it Adventure Rock. Here, in my imagination, I became a cowgirl searching for bandits or an Indian who was an expert horseback rider and knew all the signs to follow tracks in the woods. The most fun was to pretend I was a horse, running wild and free. Of course, I didn't tell Ben any of this. He'd think I was a stupid kid.

Side by side, we sat silently gazing down at the little valley. As if he were a mind reader, he said, "Me and my friends used to play cowboy-and-Indian-hide-and-seek on horseback."

My mind strayed, and I pictured us playing cowboy and damsel in distress, with Ben being like a hero in the movies, rescuing me from evil, cutthroat bank robbers.

Mama's hollering, "Winna, Winna," ruined my fabulous daydream.

I sighed. "Better get home."

Looking down at me, he curved his full lips into a smile. I raised my brows to make my eyes look wider and fluttered my lashes like Veronica did when she flirted. "Maybe the next time we ride, we can play cowboy hide-and-seek."

His smile turned into a broad grin, and he shrugged. "Sure, why not."

We hurried to crawl back through the fence. Ben laced his hands together and made a finger stirrup to help me back on Babyface. Then he swung onto his saddle and kicked Sugar into a gallop. Grasping her blonde mane, I prayed Babyface wouldn't make an abrupt detour as we dashed down the path.

Without mishap, we halted at the gate, and Ben climbed off to unlatch it and led Sugar through. I followed them to his front yard. He looked at the sky and said, "Hope it's clear like this for the fireworks tonight at the beach."

"Fireworks?" I asked. "On the beach?"

"Yeah, for the Fourth of July," Ben said. "When it's dark enough, they shoot off fireworks." His green eyes sparkled. "It's wild."

On the farm, I'd twirled a few sparklers but had never seen real fireworks. I wanted to go with him in the worst way. Mama said ladies didn't invite themselves. Hooey on all that lady stuff. I would ask, anyway. I took a deep breath to build my resolve, but before my nervousness settled down, he said, "Gotta go. See you later," and turned to unsaddle Sugar.

Looking at his back, I felt stupid and couldn't bolster up enough nerve to ask. "Bye," I said.

I rode back home, turned Babyface loose in the pasture, and then raced down the hill to tell my parents about the fireworks in hopes we could go too.

Chapter Nine
Snafu

In the kitchen, Mama stood at the stove. The minute I saw her, I asked, "Can we go to the beach to watch fireworks tonight? The kids who moved next-door are going. Please. I've never seen real fireworks."

Wiping her hands on a dishtowel, Mama turned. "I'll go over there and find out about it. Want to come?"

With an angry edge to her voice and an annoyed glint in her eyes, she appeared to be on a toot. I'd been good. What had upset her? She couldn't go to Ben's. What if she acted obnoxiously? What would he think of my family and me? He'd think my family was awful, that I was awful. That's what he'd think.

I shook my head. "It's too early in the morning to visit them. Don't bother. Fireworks are no big deal."

"Let's go." She clutched my arm and tugged. "I want to meet our new neighbors, anyway. See what kind of people have moved next door."

"No, Mama, don't go. I don't want to see the fireworks. Please!"

"You're not coming?"

"No."

She'd ruin everything. I couldn't stand to be there if she acted strange, or worse, mean and crazy in front of Ben and his family. If she made a big drunken scene, he'd never like me, and all the neighbors would know, too, including Trudy.

Snafu was a perfect word for this all fouled up situation.

Mama's fingers dug into the skin of my arm. When she got like this, sometimes things turned ugly, and there would be an argument. Usually, she only argued with Daddy, but sometimes she squabbled with neighbors. Once she cussed out a neighbor when his dog wandered onto our farm. At school the next day, some of the kids had heard about it and asked me what had happened. I couldn't think of what to say. Some of the girls laughed and whispered. I wanted to disappear like the invisible man and slink away. Looking straight ahead, I pretended not to notice their mocking eyes.

Mama glared at me with bleary eyes. Maybe I'd be lucky, and Ben's parents would think she had a disability, a lisp or something. I shook my arm from her grasp and switched on the radio. How perfect, "Heartbreak Hotel" played.

As if an electric switch turned off, Mama's mood changed from mad to sad. She sat on a yellow dinette chair, rested her elbows on her knees, covered her face with her hands, and started to weep.

Between sobs, she said, "You don't want to go. You're ashamed of me, aren't you?"

"No, no," I lied. "Want to, uh, make cornbread, that's all."

Just then, Daddy came into the kitchen. "Do I smell bacon?" He picked a piece out of the frying pan. "Looks good enough to eat."

Mama straightened in her chair, dried her eyes with her apron, and shot him a slitty-eyed look. "Of course, it is, and Winna's going to make cornbread."

Daddy nodded. "Sounds good." He sat at the table, avoided Mama's glare, munched the bacon, and began reading the newspaper.

"You sit there like a king waiting to be served," she said.

He sighed and looked up. "You must be tired. You need to rest." This was the usual excuse he made for her when she drank.

He got up and walked toward the doorway. When she didn't follow, he went to the table and coaxed her. "Come on, Sarah. I'll put a cool washcloth on your forehead. It will help your headache. After you rest, you'll feel better."

Daddy helped her up. She staggered and leaned against him. Holding her arm, he supported her as they walked out the back door and onto the porch toward their room.

Now quiet, the house seemed as empty as an unplugged bathtub. I switched on the electric oven to four hundred degrees. I mixed up cornbread and then plunged my fingers into a can of shortening, greased the muffin tins, and filled them with thick, golden batter.

I washed my greasy hands and noticed my gnawed fingernails. Nice nails were on Mama's lady list, and she badgered me to quit biting them. They did look ugly. I vowed to stop, and my new resolve for self-improvement inspired me to enter forbidden territory.

I pulled the baked cornbread out of the oven and went into my sister's bedroom. An Elvis *Love Me Tender* movie poster hung on the wall above her bed. It was her one possession I coveted most of all. Where was she, anyway? Probably at Jenny Lee's.

Veronica kept a diary. Bet she wrote good stuff in it about boys. If I read it, I'd probably learn a lot. Where did she hide it? I looked under her mattress and checked her dresser drawers. Guess she'd found a better hiding place.

Skirts, blouses, and Capri pants were scattered helter-skelter on top of the bed. Shoes were carelessly heaped in a corner. I tried to squeeze my extra-wide foot into a pair of her red flats and felt like Cinderella's stepsister.

An empty Mr. Peanut bank sat on top of her dresser along with a fingernail file, jumbled bottles of various shades of nail polish, and polish remover. The bottles were in such disarray that surely she wouldn't notice one being moved.

Hurriedly, I chose a soft pink. Then keeping alert for any sound from outside, I sat on the floor and filed my snaggity nails. I'd never painted my nails before, and it was amazingly difficult to brush on polish before it turned gooey. I wiped it off with remover and painted them three times, but my bitten-to-the-quick fingernails still looked terrible.

Polishing them took longer than I thought. A noise outside made me hurry to return everything to the exact place on the dresser to make it appear as if nothing had been touched. The front door banged as I rushed out of the bedroom.

Veronica screamed, "What were you doing in my room?"

"Uh, thought I'd be nice and straighten it for you."

Her nose twitched like a bunny's, and her eyes strayed toward her dresser. "I smell polish remover. You've been into my polish. Haven't you?"

She grabbed my hand and found evidence of my crime. With lips tightened into an ugly grimace, her face turned a horrible red, and she went berserk. Slapping at me, she grasped my arm, slung me against the wall, grabbed my hair and yanked.

I squealed and kicked as we wrestled to the floor. Veronica jerked my hair harder. I wailed louder and tried to grab her hair too.

Just about then, Mama stomped into the room, yelled, "What's going on?" and then swatted us with a fly swatter.

We rolled out of her way and managed to scramble up. Rushing past her, we ran out the front door and up the hill trail steps with Puppy in pursuit. The horses saw us hurry into the barn and trotted in too.

Babyface nosed around in the manger. Finding it empty, she raised her head and stared at me. I climbed on the haystack and threw the mares a flake of hay.

To catch my breath, I sat and dangled my legs over the edge of the stack. Veronica climbed up, sat next to me, and elbowed me in the ribs. "You know my room is off limits."

Not wanting to get into another tussle, I heaved a huge sigh, kept my temper, and said, "I shouldn't touch your stuff."

Satisfied she'd made her point and won the argument, she nodded. After a silent minute, she said, "I shouldn't have slapped you. It's not very ladylike, is it?"

I snorted like a pig. We both giggled and lay back on the hay. Puppy cuddled against me and rested her chin on my chest. While the horses chomped, my sister and I lay side-by-side, held hands, and stared at the sky through the holes in the roof.

Like Puppy's wheezy snore, a gentle breeze inhaled and exhaled through the gaps between the boards of the barn's siding. A shroud of dim light enveloped us with tranquility. The barn was a sanctuary.

Veronica rested her head on my shoulder and picked up my hand to inspect my fingernails. "Biting your nails makes them look ugly," she said. "You did a lousy job. If you'd asked, I would have painted them for you, and then at least they'd look halfway decent."

I sniffed back a tear. "I wish I had. Now, Mama's mad. Hope she doesn't nag Daddy into getting rid of the horses."

"Don't worry. When she's like this, the next day she's forgotten everything."

"Except, I wanted to see fireworks at the beach tonight."

Veronica did a quick sit-up. "Fireworks? At the beach tonight? If we ask Daddy, he'll say yes." She clambered down from the stack, and I hurried to keep up with her as she jogged down the hill.

Chapter Ten
Racehorse

We warily entered the kitchen where Mama sat with one elbow propped on the table, resting her probably aching forehead in the palm of her hand. Before we could disappear from the room, she straightened in her chair. Pulling a pack of cigarettes from her pocket, she stuck one between her lips, lit a match and puffed, and then inhaled deeply.

With a sigh, she exhaled, and smoke billowed around her face. Her piercing eyes focused on me. "Well, at least you made cornbread. I'll go tell your daddy breakfast is ready." She stood and took uneven, tottery steps out to the screened porch.

"Dear God, please, let her be over her snit and not complain to Daddy about the horses," I whispered, hoping going to church with Mrs. Barr every Sunday had won me prayer points.

The house was quiet, not even a creak, except for Veronica's growling stomach. She got up to scramble eggs while I set plates on the table, along with the cornbread muffins still in the tin and a dish of butter.

"Thought I heard someone cooking," Daddy said as he came into the kitchen. Making a big show of sniffing, he sat at the table with us.

We had about finished breakfast when Veronica, in a fake sweet-little-girl voice, asked, "Can we go see fireworks at the beach tonight?"

Not looking up, Daddy took the last corn muffin and shook his head. "Fireworks? No. Not tonight. Your mother's too tired to go tonight."

When Mama drank too much, Daddy made excuses for her, like she was worn out or had a difficult day. He'd pretend nothing was wrong.

"I can drive," Veronica said in a voice changed from drippy sweet to a soft whine. "You and Mama don't have to go." She smiled a smile so warm and tender it could have melted the butter Daddy spread on his cornbread. "I promise to be really, really careful. *Pleeease.*"

She kicked me under the table.

"Please, Daddy," I piped in. "I've never seen fireworks before, and the new kids next door are going."

"Met our new neighbors yesterday," he said. "They seem like good people. The dad's the new manager of a bar and restaurant that just opened." Daddy looked down and squinted as he often did when considering. He chewed and then swallowed a mouthful of coffee before nodding. "Okay, with one condition. I'm trusting you to get home the minute the fireworks are over. No joyriding around after."

Veronica's cheeks blushed pink with excitement. She leaped up and hugged him. "We won't. I promise."

The phone rang three times, then a pause, which was our party-line ring. I snatched up the receiver to answer before my sister could.

"It's for me." I pressed the black receiver against my ear and imagined Trudy sitting in her sunny new kitchen at the other end of the line.

"What happened to you yesterday?" Trudy asked. "Why didn't you come back to my house so we could go riding?"

"Uh, well, sorry. I was so excited, I forgot. When I got home, guess what? Snafu had her foal. A beautiful little filly. We named her Chaos."

"What a cute name. Can't wait to see her."

"Maybe in a few days. Daddy warned us Snafu might get angry protecting her new foal." I switched listening ears. "And yesterday, a family with kids moved next door. The oldest is a teenage boy. Really cute too. We're going to the beach to watch fireworks tonight." Pretending Ben had asked me to go with him wasn't exactly a lie.

"Cute, huh. Is he nice too?" Trudy asked.

"Think so. Nice, gorgeous, and has a horse."

"He has a horse? How cool."

Her voice sounded funny, jealous, maybe. I waited for her to ask more about Ben. After a quiet second, she said, "Come over and keep me company while I clean my room. Then we can ride."

"Sure. I'll be over in a while."

To keep Daddy happy, I helped him wash our breakfast dishes. Together, we cleared the table. He softly whistled "Amazing Grace" while I washed, and he dried and put the plates in the cupboard. Daddy was the rock of our family. He tried to make everything okay when Mama was out of sorts, as he called it.

When we'd finished cleaning up, he folded the dishtowel, then turned to me and gently squeezed my shoulder. "I don't want your mother worried, so don't be out too late tonight." Lines on his forehead seemed deeper, and his eyes looked weary when he patted the top of my head. "In a few days, we'll catch the filly and halter break her."

"I fed the horses," I said. "Can I ride over to Trudy's?"

Daddy nodded and smooched my forehead.

I went into the bathroom, and my reflection in the small mirror revealed what I already knew. My growing-out hair was an impossible mess. I'd always wanted hair long enough to pull into a ponytail, but Mama made me cut it short because long hair was too much trouble. Now I was a teenager, and no matter what Mama said, I was letting it grow. Tonight, my hair had to look good. If it were curled, maybe it'd look at least halfway decent.

Veronica knew how to do great pin curls. I peeked into her room. She lay in bed, head propped on a pillow, reading *Peyton Place*. The book's cover had a few large greasy spots, but otherwise, it appeared to have survived the trashcan.

At my own risk, I entered her sacred territory. She looked up and then quickly flicked her eyes back down to the page.

"Will you help me pin curl my hair?"

"Not now. Maybe later. I'm reading a good part."

Which meant she was reading the parts with lots of juicy kissing. Her eyes were glued to the page. I sighed, but she still didn't look up. I sighed again, more loudly. No response.

"Okay, gator, later."

The morning was still cool around 11:00. By now, Bakersfield would have started baking. Up in the barn, the horses were still eating their breakfast. The rough-sawn boards on the manger's edge had worn smooth over the years. It made a perfect place to sit while the horses munched.

Snafu ignored me while Chaos cautiously watched from behind her.

Maybe talking would help them get used to me hanging around.

"Mama's got one of her headaches," I told them. "It couldn't be helping Daddy feel better. She acts worried about him, but if she truly cared, she'd stop drinking."

Telling about Daddy being sick worried me. To cheer up, I decided to talk about something happy and said, "Good thing Veronica can drive. Tonight, we're going to see fireworks. They'll be fantastic, but you probably wouldn't like them."

In the quiet barn, the only sound was the horses crunchy chewing. They did not appear the least interested in cars or fireworks.

I decided to hike to Trudy's while Babyface ate her breakfast. Hearing my knock, Trudy opened her bedroom window. "The door's not locked. Come on in."

I sat on her bed and watched her organize her closet, color-coordinating her clothes: red skirts hang with red blouses, blue with blue, yellow with yellow.

She stood back, admired her orderly closet, and said, "I can hardly wait to get new school clothes. I want a poodle skirt in the worst way. Do you have one?"

"No. They are so cool, though," I said, even though poodle skirts were dumb, and I'd never be caught wearing one.

Trudy sat by me and said, "Can you believe Elvis is being drafted? Won't it be terrible?"

I nodded, even though not sure why it would be. He and I would have something in common. His bedspread would be an ugly army blanket like mine.

Trudy jabbered on about her favorite movie stars, sorted through a laundry basket full of pink undies and bras, folded them neatly, and then placed everything in perfect rows inside her dresser drawers.

It was boring watching her dust princess furniture. Then she dragged a vacuum cleaner into her room. Before she could turn it on and suck balls of lint out from under her pink ruffled canopy bed, I said, "I'm going home to groom Babyface. Hurry up so we can ride. Maybe Ben will ride with us."

"I'm almost finished. When I'm done, I'll ride Blackie over."

On my way home, a girl skipped up. She flipped a long braid over her shoulder, then tilted her head up to peer at me. Cat-eye-framed glasses magnified her green eyes like Mr. Magoo's.

"I'm Tina, Ben's sister. Was that your dad at our house yesterday?"

"Guess so. I'm Winna. Want to go up to the pasture with me and see my horse?"

Wrinkling her nose up in an I-smell-sour-milk sort of way, she said, "Don't like them."

I shook my head in disbelief. What was wrong with her? What a dope. How could anyone not like horses? "Well, uh, anyway, do you think Ben wants to ride?"

"He's doing chores." Tina studied my face with those gigantic eyes. "You like Ben, huh?"

My face felt hot under her scrutiny. It must be glowing pink.

Seeing me squirm, she smugly said, "I'll tell him you asked about him." Then she turned and skipped toward her house, singing, *"You ain't nothin' but a hotdog."*

Gads, what a pain, she had ruined Elvis's song.

In the barn, the mares' muzzles were still burrowed in the manger. While brushing Babyface's dusty coat, I told her she was beautiful and picked twigs from her tail. She was slick and shiny by the time I rode next door where Trudy sat on Blackie, finger twirling her blonde ponytail and chatting with Ben.

Even though Trudy wore those ugly braces, Ben probably thought she was pretty. He saw me and said, "Hey, Winna."

Trudy nodded a hello, and then kicked the toes of her brand new red cowboy boots out of her stirrups. I'd like to have seen how she'd managed to saddle Blackie.

"Want to ride with us?" she asked Ben.

"Dad said if I wanted to see the fireworks tonight, I had to finish my chores."

Trudy traced circles on her saddle horn with a perfectly manicured fingernail, gave Ben a shy glance, and hinted, "I'd love to see the fireworks."

He shrugged. "Yeah. They're something to see all right. Well, gotta finish my chores. See you later."

Ben's t-shirt stretched across his broad shoulders as he retreated toward his backyard. I sighed and said, "Come on, Trudy. Let's ride to the beach and see what's happening."

She huffed a sigh too. "Yes, sure, let's."

Was she jealous because she thought I was going with Ben tonight? If she were, I wouldn't blame her. Except, if we both had a crush on him, it would be tough being friends. I should invite her to go with Veronica and me. Except how could I without her realizing I'd pretended and really wasn't going with Ben to the beach?

Hmmm? Why not make her think I'd decided to go with Veronica in our new car instead. Acting all giddy, I said, "Guess what? Daddy said Veronica could drive our new Chevy to see the fireworks. Cool, huh? Want to go with us?"

When Trudy grinned, her lips scraped over her gleaming braces. "Oh, yes," she said. "I'll ask my mom."

We rode through town, and the plate glass window of Louise's Dress Shop mirrored our reflections. I looked taller and more important riding Babyface and remembered what Mrs. Barr told me about local happenings. "Hey, in the fall, there's a Harvest Festival parade right through town. Wouldn't it be neat to ride in it? We could dress like Annie Oakley."

"That would be cool," Trudy said as she gazed at her reflection too.

Passing the churches, we crossed over railroad tracks and rode through the dunes that sheltered the town from ocean breezes. We came to the long stretch of beach where families had already gathered, staking out the best places to watch the fireworks. As we rode by, kids ran up, wanting to pet the horses, or yelled stupid things like "Ride 'em, cowgirl!"

Dodging giant clumps of seaweed, we rode into the surf. Foamy-white water swirled around the horses' legs like soap suds and scared them. We urged them forward and got showered with cold ocean spray. A bit dizzy from the ebb and flow of the waves, we turned the horses toward home.

On the way, we took a shortcut, Stagecoach Road. Unpaved, it made a perfect racetrack. Trudy yelled, "Let's race," and kicked Blackie into a run.

Babyface jumped out fast and passed Blackie like Man o' War. I leaned over her neck like a jockey and grasped her mane tight enough to pull it out by the roots. Fence posts whizzed by as I tugged on the reins. She bowed her neck, clenched her mouth against the bit, and raced at top speed, not slowing down at all. With hoofs clattering on the hard-packed road, she ran toward home.

Ahead, the dirt road narrowed into a brushy downhill trail. My heart drummed as loud as Babyface's pounding hoofs. Huge squirrel holes lurked underfoot. I hung on, terrified she'd step into one of those enormous holes, break her leg, and crash to the ground. Coyote brush slapped my face as she galloped like a whirlwind down the steep hill.

Once clear of the brush, the ground leveled, and Babyface raced toward the bean field, where she twirled, missing a row of staked beans by inches. I took a kamikaze nosedive, and abruptly she stopped, turned her head, and innocently gaze back at me lying in the black mud.

Recovering my senses but trembling, I hoisted myself up from the ground and looked down at my mud-covered clothes. "Babyface, you're crazy," I hollered. "You could have killed us!"

Hot breath snorted from her nostrils. I grabbed her dragging reins and steadied myself against her sweaty neck while we both caught our breath. With nothing to use to climb on, I led her back to find Trudy, who walked a calm Blackie along the trail.

Trudy stood a moment with her mouth agape, then said, "What happened?"

"Couldn't stop. Did a quick dismount at the bean field. Man, Babyface is fast." My voice still trembled from the gallons of adrenalin that had pumped through my veins. I wanted to save face and faked a giggle to pretend my fall didn't matter.

Shrugging, Trudy wrinkled her nose and gave a patronizing sniff. "She may be fast, but running out of control proves she isn't well trained. Blackie stopped when I asked her."

Trudy's mouth must have tasted awful from eating all those sour grapes. "Listen, don't be telling your mom we raced or that Babyface ran away with me. If Daddy thought she wasn't safe to ride, he'd sell her."

She shot me a don't-be-stupid look. "I won't tell. If my mom found out we raced, she'd be angry too. But maybe your dad should sell Babyface and buy you a well-trained horse like Blackie."

"Yep. Babyface isn't a good stopper." I laughed, trying not to show how irked I was by her snotty attitude. Even though Babyface was faster and Blackie lost the race, Trudy wanted me to think her horse was better.

Now she had two reasons to be jealous, Ben and my speedy racehorse.

"I'm a muddy mess," I said. "Better get going. Call me if you can't go. Otherwise, we'll be at your house around 7:00."

Chapter Eleven
Fireworks

As I led Babyface home, she walked quietly. Back at the barn, I threw hay in the manger, and Snafu and Chaos galloped in. Eager to get ready to see the fireworks, I didn't take time to brush or talk to them. At the water trough, I washed the mud off the best I could.

On the back porch, I took off my wet clothes and threw them in the washing machine. While I soaked in the bath, pots and pans clattered in the kitchen. Mama probably had a tiff with Daddy. Or was she mad because I left a mess on the porch? I was glad the kitchen was empty by the time I got out of the tub.

I had to do something with my hair. Usually, I didn't spend much time fixing it, but tonight I wanted to look special. I'd be glad when it grew long enough to brush into a ponytail.

My sister wasn't in her room. With the bobby pins scattered on her dresser, I attempted to pin curl my hair. No matter how hard I tried, wisps of hair sprung out. I gave up, combed my bangs flat, and tried to hide the mess under a scarf but looked like the little match girl.

Plastering my wet hair behind my ears, I clipped it back with a pair of Veronica's silver barrettes, hoping when it dried, even though it wouldn't look great, it might look okay.

Waiting for my sister to get home, I thumbed through a fashion magazine lying on the floor next to her bed. Teenage models in the pictures had perfect hair and perfect clothes. My sister said a girl had to wear stylish clothes to be popular. I went into my room and dug through my cramped closet filled with boring shirtwaist dresses. I didn't think they'd qualify as the wardrobe to win a popularity contest.

I shoved them aside and found a powder blue shirt stained with only a few green sprinkles from one of Billy's gigantic horse sneezes. In the dark, the stains wouldn't be too noticeable. I kept hunting and found an old pair of pedal pushers. Would blue go with brown-and-white stripes? I tried them on to see how they looked. Not terrible, but they didn't look good either.

Hmmm? Maybe I'd better wear my sneeze blouse with jeans.

It was almost 6:30 before the back door slammed. In the kitchen, Veronica scrounged for leftovers in the refrigerator. Jenny Lee sat at the table, wearing short shorts that exposed every inch of her long, freckled legs.

Veronica glued her eyes on me. "Are those my barrettes?"

"Without your help, I couldn't curl my hair," I said. "May I wear them? Please."

Before she answered, Daddy came in. Was Mama sleeping it off? He placed his hands on his hips and said, "Remember what I told you." Then he dropped the Chevy's key in Veronica's outstretched hand.

"Thank you." Her fingers curled around the keys, and before he changed his mind about letting us go, we grabbed our jackets and hurried outside.

I started to climb into the front seat, and Veronica shook her head. She gave me a don't-do-it squint and pointed to the back, and Jenny Lee jumped in front. After settling into the backseat, I said, "I invited Trudy. Told her we'd pick her up."

The Chevy's engine purred as we navigated Trudy's steep driveway. When Veronica honked, Trudy opened her front door and yelled, "I'm coming." Within a minute, she hurried out, pulling on a sweater, and got in the back seat with me. Her ponytail twisted into a perfect curly twirl, she wore a frilly-collared white blouse with cute red pedal pushers, which made me feel even tackier wearing a pair of old rolled-up jeans, with my hair clamped down with barrettes.

We couldn't find a space at the beach or in the churches' parking lots and ended up parking along the street. We only toted our jackets, but many people trekked over the dunes carrying blankets, baskets, ice chests, folding chairs, and babies. We got to the beach, and I scanned the crowd for Ben. I spotted him, and we weaved through the maze of people sitting on chairs or huge towels to where he and his father were spreading their blankets.

I tapped his shoulder.

He turned, and surprised when he saw it was me, said, "Hey, Winna."

Under his sister's magnified-eyeball scrutiny, I stood like a dope, trying to think of something intelligent to say. Then his eyes darted toward Veronica.

She gave him the full-flirt treatment. She tilted her chin, lowered her gaze, and fluttered her thick veil of black lashes. Then, in a voice she never used except with handsome boys, she said, "Hi, Ben. I'm Winna's sister, Veronica." Then as an afterthought, she said, "And this is Jenny Lee and Trudy."

Now that Ben had met my sister, with her dimpled chin and long lashes fringing her sultry eyes, I wouldn't stand a chance with him.

After we all helped spread their blankets, Ben's mother stopped digging through baskets and invited us to sit with them to watch the fireworks. Except, it was still twilight, and we'd have to wait until dark for the fireworks to begin.

People gathered around blazing driftwood bonfires, and bratty kids jumped around, kicking sand. Ben searched their picnic basket and pulled out a bag of marshmallows and toasting sticks. "Come on. Let's toast some."

We pushed through the crowd and stood next to a bonfire. Trudy twisted a stray lock of hair, coyly lowered her eyes, and asked Ben to help her slide a marshmallow onto her stick. It sickened me watching her play the helpless girl.

I shoved a soft marshmallow on a stick and melted the white blob into a black, crispy glob. Plucking and eating the gooey sugar glued onto our sticks made our hands and mouths sticky. We all dashed into the ocean waves to wash off, except for Trudy, who stayed out of the water because she didn't want to get her new pants wet.

Ben started a water fight with Veronica. We all laughed and joined in, splashing each other. My lips tasted salty-sweet as I licked the seawater dripping down my face.

We ran back to the bonfire to get warm and dry, and Jenny Lee longingly eyed Ben's picnic basket. His mom must have noticed and offered us wieners to roast on our sticks.

After sizzling a wiener over the fire, I crammed it on a hotdog bun and squirted on ketchup and mustard. Jenny Lee rushed to sit on the blanket next to Ben. In disgust, I almost gagged on a mouthful of bread when she stretched out her legs, heaved a sigh, and thrust out her ample chest like the women on the calendars in mechanics' shops.

I sat on the other side of Ben, and Veronica and Trudy huddled close behind me. Veronica shoved her toes under my butt and giggled. Ignoring her, I munched my hotdog, drank Kool-Aid, and stared at the sky, waiting for the shower of lights to begin.

A brilliant burst of red, white, and blue spider-webbed across the sky as if cans of paint had exploded in heaven. The crowd "oohed" and "ahhed" at every blast. While everyone gazed up, I peeked over at Ben just as he looked down at me.

The brilliant colors of the fireworks danced over his face and kissable lips. Embarrassed, I jerked my staring eyes away and pretended to be interested in the show of bright lights in the sky. I was glad it was dark. My hot face had probably turned the color of a boiled lobster.

When the fireworks were over, Veronica and Jenny Lee wandered down the beach toward a group of people huddled around a huge bonfire. Trudy and I helped Ben and his mom pack the baskets, shake the sand from the blankets, and fold them.

Ben hoisted the picnic basket onto his shoulder. "See ya," he said. Then with his family, he trudged through the sand toward the parking lot.

Trudy and I hurried along the shoreline to find Veronica and Jenny Lee. They stood warming their backsides by a huge crackling and popping blaze hot enough to singe my eyebrows. Just outside the fire's glare, some of the group sat on blankets, kissing and drinking beer.

"Ya want a beer?" Jenny Lee asked.

Veronica's eyes glowed in the firelight like some trouble-making pixie. She gave a slight nod. Jenny Lee returned the nod and then nonchalantly strolled over to an ice chest, looked around, and lifted the lid.

Before she could swipe one, a large girl with jet-black hair said in a gravelly mean voice, "Who said you could have a beer?"

Everyone turned to look.

The girl slammed the lid down. Before it whapped shut, Jenny Lee managed to jerk her hand out of the chest. She straightened her shoulders, shoved her face into the girl's, and said, "Myself and me, that's who!"

The girl, three inches taller, didn't buffalo. She grabbed Jenny Lee's hair and jerked.

Jenny Lee screamed and punched the girl.

Like a swarm of wasps after blood, a crowd rushed over, chanting, "Fight. Fight. Fight."

I clutched Veronica's wrist. "Come on. Let's get out of here." I tugged, but she wouldn't budge. Riveted to the spot, she tried to yank her wrist out of my grasp.

I let go of her, and Trudy and I hurried down the beach, away from the uproar. As we ran, what sounded like police sirens screamed in the dunes behind us.

When we were far enough from the commotion, we stopped and looked back. Red lights flashed in the beach parking lot. No longer cheering and laughing, the crowd had scattered.

Veronica and Jenny Lee ran toward us. They plopped down in the sand next to me, panting to catch their breath. After about ten minutes, the wailing sirens trailed off.

Jenny Lee held her stomach in a belly laugh. "Wow. That was a close one."

"Violating the law is not funny," Trudy said.

"Oh...Really, Miss Priss? Well, Ha. Ha. Ha."

Jenny Lee was so stupid she thought her fake laugh made her look smart. Veronica needed to ditch juvie girl before she got her in big trouble.

Chapter Twelve
The Saddle

The ringing telephone woke me. With cobwebs still in my brain, I hurried to answer it. Trudy's voice gushed with excitement. "Mom said an ambulance brought a man into the emergency room last night who got badly burned setting off fireworks."

It took a second to register what she'd said. "So, the police weren't at the beach last night because of Jenny Lee's fight?"

"Probably not." Trudy lip-smacked a tsk. "But wasn't it terrible how she acted like a juvenile delinquent."

"Well, uh, yeah, she's nutty. She's apt to--"

"Anyways," Trudy interrupted. "What I called to tell you is one of the ambulance drivers told Mom a horse trainer operates a tack shop at a ranch on our road. Do you want to ride over and help me shop for a new saddle?"

"Sure. Come over and we'll go."

Before I'd even changed out of my PJs, Trudy was outside on Blackie, yelling, "Winna. Winna."

"Hold your horses. I'll be out in a minute," I hollered out the front door.

"Hurry up."

Slipping off my pajamas, I pulled on jeans, wiggled a shirt on over my head, combed a few rats out of my hair, and then pulled on my dirty white sneakers, leaving a note before rushing out. Trudy followed me to the pasture gate, and the mares galloped over to nose Blackie, making it easy to catch Babyface. I bridled her and led her beside the water trough to jump on. Trudy was in such a rush she rode off before I'd settled on Babyface's back, and I barely managed to keep my balance as she trotted off.

On the way, for some reason, Babyface decided to walk in the middle of the road. Her hoofs clip-clopped on the hard pavement. I urged her to move off to the side where it was safe, but she ignored me and continued to amble along. Good thing there wasn't any traffic.

A herd of mares and foals were pastured where a sign along the road read: *Sweet Springs Ranch-Arabians for Sale*. When we turned into the ranch's driveway, the horses spotted us and snorted and pranced alongside the fence, arching their necks, flaring their nostrils, and raising their tails high. The foals appeared to float when they trotted as if tiny wings were on their heels.

At the end of the driveway, inside a round corral, a cowboy loped a chestnut horse in a circle. He saw us, slid the mare to a stop, and said, "Need help?"

"Do you have a saddle shop?" Trudy asked.

The cowboy dismounted, opened the corral gate, and led the mare to us. His white cowboy hat shaded a wrinkled, leathery face that looked a hundred years old. He gazed up at me with milky brown eyes. "Sure do. I'm Joseph. Got a little tack shop in the barn. Come on, I'll show ya."

He led his horse to the barn and then pointed. "You can tie your horses there."

We tied them to the hitching post and followed him into the barn. His hands were as gnarled and wrinkled as his face, but he nimbly loosened the cinch strap, pulled the saddle off, and moved easily to place it on a rack. After silently brushing the mare, he turned her into a stall filled with clean smelling straw. After hanging the halter on a peg next to the stall door, he said, "Okay, now, what ya need?"

Trudy's words poured out in a rush. "I'm looking for a saddle. Mom says I can buy a new one and a new matching headstall for my bridle."

Joseph raised his brows. "Is that so? Well, then, let's have a look-see."

He walked to the end of the barn aisle, unlatched a door, and flipped on a light. The pungent smell of oiled leather filled the small tack room. Racks of saddles lined one wall, and I couldn't resist touching the polished leather. Gads, I wanted a new saddle, too.

Rows of shiny bits hung on the wall opposite the saddles. Some looked ordinary and dull gray like mine, but some silver with mouthpieces looked like spoons with copper rollers. My finger traced over the curlicues etched on the silver shank of one of the bits. "Your bits are beautiful. You have so many. Do you use all of them?"

Joseph tipped back his hat and squinted. "Well, ya see, every horse's mouth is shaped different and needs a bit that fits it. Then he'll work his best."

"My horse ran away with me and wouldn't stop 'til she got home," I said. "Maybe I don't have the right one."

The old cowboy cocked his head and looked at me. "You're a little girl. Maybe ya need somethin' that'll make her listen to ya. With more of a mouthpiece than that grazin' bit you're usin'." He selected a bit and offered it to me. "Maybe this one might help ya get your tall mare under control."

I took the bit, twirled the roller inside the high-curved mouthpiece, and it chirped like a cricket. "It sounds neat-o. Guess I'll need to learn all about bits to be a horse trainer."

"Ya wanna train horses?" Joseph pulled a red handkerchief out of his pocket and blew his nose with a loud honk. "There ain't much call for horse trainers no more. The big ranches around here are mostly gone. Not much need for cowboys nowadays. Exceptin' horse show people want their horses trained for showin'. They do have fine horses, finer than the mustangs I used to train. Those were wild-bred horses. No pedigrees like the ones on this here ranch. But they were doin' horses, and their hearts were just as big."

"I was thinking about training horses for the circus." I twirled the bit's roller again to hear it chirp. "We have a brand new filly, only a few days old. I'm going to help Daddy halter break her and teach her how to lead. Right now, I'm trying to make friends with her."

Joseph stared at his cracked, scuffed boots. "The circus, huh? Well, startin' 'em young is best. Easier. Spend lots of time, pay attention, and you'll learn to understand your filly. She'll teach ya to think like a horse." He raised his eyes and studied the sky. "And ya can't show fear. A horse smells fear and then's afraid, too. Never use your whip in anger. Then she won't trust ya and won't never be your friend."

Okay, so to win Chaos's friendship and be able to start halter breaking her, I needed to pay attention, learn to think like a horse, be kind, and never get mad, even if she shoved me in a pile of horse crap. To make friends, I had to be a friend, which would be easier to do with Chaos than with some people.

While Joseph and I talked, Trudy gawked at all of the saddles. "I like this one," she said, pointing to one with a design that looked like a basket woven in leather. "Do you think it is the right size for me?"

Joseph carried a saddle rack into the center of the room and placed the saddle on it so Trudy could test it. "Climb up there and see."

She threw her right leg over the saddle, grinned, and wiggled her rump until satisfied it sat in the perfect spot. "I love it. I'll bring Mom to see it."

"Let's see if it fits your mare first." The old cowboy picked up the saddle and toted it outside to try on Blackie. While he helped Trudy, I admired the saddles inside the shop. One had flowers patterned in the leather, even on the saddle horn. I tried to pick it up, and it wasn't very heavy. This was the one I wanted.

When Joseph and Trudy returned, I asked, "Can I try this one?"

"Sure can. I'll put it on the saddle rack for ya."

I climbed up and sat as tall as I could. It was perfect. The stirrups were even the right length. "It's made for ya," Joseph said. "Want to try it on your horse?"

"Daddy didn't say I could buy a saddle."

"Well, it won't hurt to try it on your mare, just in case." Joseph carried the saddle outside, threw it on Babyface's back, tightened the cinch, and checked the fit. Then he led her in a circle and tightened the cinch again before he said, "Looks okay. Climb up."

Standing on my tiptoes, I stretched my leg high enough for my foot to reach the stirrup and then grasped the long tie-strings to hoist myself up. This time the saddle stayed put. My feet felt perfect in the wide stirrups. The flower imprinted on the saddle horn was beautiful. I envied Trudy.

I sighed. "I do like it. I'll ask Daddy if I can get it." I kicked my feet out of the stirrups and slowly slid to the ground. "Thank you for letting me try the saddle."

"Now, let's trade bits on your bridle." Joseph took Babyface's bridle off and then put a halter on her. He unsaddled her and took everything back into the tack shop. Then with sure fingers, he buckled another bit on her headstall.

Back outside, he slid his hand gently down Babyface's nose and slipped the new bit into her mouth. She smacked her lips, and the copper roller clicked. "Tastes good, eh?" Joseph said and then turned to me. "See if this one don't work better."

"Thanks. I'll ask Daddy about the saddle."

Joseph laced his hands together into a stirrup to help me climb on. Once on top of Babyface's now bare back, I looked down. He grinned, and deep wrinkles folded around his eyes like dried leather. "Keep workin' with the horses. That's how you'll learn." He patted Babyface, gave a wave, and then turned and briskly walked into the barn.

On the ride home, Babyface tried to walk in the road again. I pulled on the reins, and this time, she moved to the side the way I wanted. The new bit worked. Old Joseph sure knew about horse training.

Trudy chattered endlessly about Joseph's tack. "Wasn't his saddles beautiful? Mom is sure to like the one I picked."

Wasn't Trudy lucky? Could I convince Daddy to buy me a new saddle too? Mama wouldn't want him to spend money without a good reason. We already had one, and she'd probably say we didn't need two.

Even so, safety was a big concern to Daddy. I could tell him it was almost impossible for me to lift our heavy saddle onto Babyface, and we needed a lighter one. It would be easier to get on her with stirrups and riding in a saddle was way safer. Except, I wouldn't say she dumped me off with fast turns.

At our driveway, I veered off the road and gave Trudy a goodbye wave. Up in the pasture, I slid off Babyface, and it felt like needles stung my cold feet when they touched the ground. I fed the horses and then hunkered down in a dim corner of the barn to watch them and learn. Ignoring me, they snorted, sneezed, and chomped their hay. It seemed that learning to think like a horse required me to enjoy food. Well, that would be easy.

Chaos kept her eyes on me and didn't come close. I told her, "Someday, you'll look pretty wearing that flowery saddle I want, won't you?"

It was cozy in the barn, talking with the horses. I could tell them anything. They'd never judge me. I stayed there a while to get Chaos used to me, then went outside and noticed squares drawn around the barnyard. Boots with ridged soles had left prints into the soft dirt. Daddy didn't wear that kind of boot. He wouldn't have left those prints. Besides, why would he be up here tramping around, drawing lines?

Chaos came out of the barn to watch me. "Have you seen someone?" I asked her. "Has someone been bothering you?"

When I got to the house, the kitchen smelled of corned beef and cabbage. Mama stood hunched over the sink, and when the back door slammed behind me, she turned. With a dour expression painted on her face, she said, "How many times do I have to tell you? Ladies don't slam doors."

"Sorry. I was excited. Someone's been snooping around the barnyard."

She dried her hands on a dishtowel and hung it on the towel rack next to the sink. "Mr. Buck came this morning to get his antiques and searched around the barn with a metal detector."

"Bet he was hunting for stage robber loot hidden in the barn," I said.

Mama shook her head. "You've got a big imagination. A bunch of junk is all you'll find in that old barn. Go out front and tell them lunch is ready, then come back and help me set the table."

Outside, Veronica giggled as she sat on the front steps with Ben. It was irritating having a sister like a brightly feathered bluebird while I was a plain brown sparrow. With her around, Ben would never notice me.

"Mama says come in. Lunch is ready. Where's Daddy?"

Veronica pointed toward the side of the house.

"Guess I better go." Ben stood, smiling with teeth so white and straight he could be in a toothpaste commercial.

"Why don't you stay for lunch?" I asked.

He didn't answer, just grinned and mesmerized me with his green-eyed gaze. I gave myself a mental kick and hurried around the house to tell Daddy and Mr. Buck lunch was ready.

When I went back into the house, Ben helped Veronica put an extra leaf in the dinette table. I set out plates and silverware, and Mama placed platters of food on the table.

Veronica quickly sat next to Ben. After everyone was seated, Mama excused herself and went into the living room. I passed Ben the cornbread. He took a piece, buttered it, and then set it on his plate next to a big slice of juicy corned beef.

Mr. Buck, sitting across from me, wiped his mouth before placing his napkin on his lap and then twirled his handlebar mustache back into stiff points. While filling his plate with a pile of soggy cabbage, he said, "Ben, my boy, can't thank you enough for helping load my trailer."

Under droopy brows, Mr. Buck's gray eyes darted around the table as he told us about his Egyptian travels as an amateur archeologist and his many treasure hunting adventures.

I'd read about Egypt. Traveling there to see the pyramids, King Tut's tomb, and all those mummies would be exciting. Since Joseph said there was no demand for horse trainers, maybe I should rethink my goals and aspirations and study archeology. Of course, I'd have to pass ninth grade first.

Maybe I could do both, be a part-time circus performer and a part-time archeologist. Bet I could start learning about it right here. Probably lots of old Indian stuff was buried around Adventure Rock.

After swallowing a mouthful of cornbread, I asked, "Mr. Buck, have you found Indian arrowheads in our pasture?"

"Can't say I've ever found anything, but the Chumash Indians lived all around hereabouts."

"Let's hunt for arrowheads tomorrow," I said, looking toward Ben. "I know some good places to search. There's a mound of chalk rocks piled on the back hill of the pasture. Something or someone could be buried there."

Mr. Buck laughed. "That's the true archeologist spirit."

With a smile, Daddy nodded. "When I was a kid, I loved digging around for buried treasure."

The platters were passed again. Ben took another slice of meat and said, "I read about California Indians in school. Finding arrowheads or stone tools would be cool."

"Stone tools?" I said.

"The Indians used stone tools. You can tell them from ordinary rocks 'cause they're chipped and shaped for cutting and grinding." Ben chewed a hunk of meat while talking. He hadn't read Mama's good manner's list.

Veronica's brow knitted into a knot, and her squinty eyes drilled into mine. Then she pasted a sweet expression on her face, turned toward Ben, and in her nicey-nice-girl voice said, "I'd love to hunt for arrowheads. Then you could teach me all about Indians."

Wouldn't you know it? Veronica was now fascinated by archeology. Faking a smile, I glared at her. "Digging for arrowheads might ruin your fingernails."

Her lips clamped. She wiped them with a napkin and said, "Not a worry. It'll be fun."

I wanted to slap my sister.

Chapter Thirteen
Footprints

The brilliant moonlight streaming through my window and the anticipation of going on a treasure hunt kept me awake. My head covered with the army blanket, I listened as the house creaked and groaned like an old lady and tried to fall asleep. About fifteen minutes had passed when a shuffling noise came from Veronica's room. I crawled out of bed and hardly made a sound as I crept into her bedroom and found her changing out of her pajamas into jeans.

"Where are you going?" I whispered.

"Sneaking out to meet Jenny Lee."

"If you get caught, you'll be in huge trouble."

"Shut up, and I won't," she said in a whispery growl. Then with only a slight creak as the screen opened, she crawled out her window.

I tiptoed to my room and got back into bed. Why did Veronica always do dumb stuff that might cause Mama to pitch a fit and say we weren't acting like young ladies and demand Daddy sell the horses because we weren't responsible?

What was she up to anyway? I had to find out, or I'd never fall asleep. Yanking on my cutoffs, I stealthily navigated the living room. The front door squeaked when I opened it, and once outside, I checked Mama and Daddy's bedroom window at the back of the house.

Whew! No light had switched on.

Night walking felt different from day walking. The air was cool and elating, charged with the possibility of unknown and exciting happenings. A dog howled, and a million stars twinkled. If I still believed in wishing on stars, which would I choose to wish on?

Maybe Veronica lied and was meeting Ben. I wandered to his house, slinked under the avocado tree, and sat beneath its dark umbrella. I started to gnaw a fingernail, but my nails were raw, bitten to the quick, so I stopped. I'd never have pretty girly-nails if I didn't break the habit.

Dry leaves crunched under Puppy's paws when she wandered under the tree to sit with me. She wagged her tail and leaves swished and crackled.

"Shhh," I said and wrapped my arms around her neck.

Puppy's wet nose and tongue swabbed my cheek with kisses. With her here, I felt safer. When I was about six, a mean neighbor dog threatened me, and even though it was way bigger than Puppy, she stood beside me, growled, and protected me.

She was the sweetest dog in the whole world, more than a dog, more like a good mother, loving and comforting me whenever I was afraid or lonely. If wishes did come true, it would be great if people were kinder and Mama loved me as much as Puppy does?

After we sat in the dark for a while, I said to her, "Come on. Nothing's happening." We walked toward the road. I entered the bean forest to give us cover and peered across the street. Was Veronica wandering around out here somewhere? Nothing was moving around outside, and all the windows at Jenny Lee's house were dark, and so were the Barrs' windows next door.

I scanned the dark yards across the road. Puppy scratched her ears, got bored, and fell asleep. Before I did too, a light switched on in the Barrs' back yard. Whoa. Was something up?

"What's goin' on out there?" someone yelled, probably Mr. Barr, and a door slammed. I squatted down and held my breath. From the shadows, two people hurried out of the Barrs' back yard. Sneakered footsteps slapped the pavement as they ran across the road.

Now alert, Puppy perked up her ears as Veronica and Jenny Lee rushed by and hid in a bean row directly behind us. If Mr. Barr came this way, he'd think it was me sneaking around his yard.

With me following her, Puppy squeezed through the stringed vines and scared the crapola out of Veronica. She sighed with relief when she realized it was me and grasped my arm and shushed me. We hunkered down until the Barrs' back porch light turned off. Then she asked, "What are you doing out here?"

"What do you mean me? What are you doing snooping around the Barrs' house in the middle of the night?"

"Having fun," Jenny Lee said, then giggled.

Veronica wagged her head. "Only an idiot would think it was fun to break into the Barrs' garage. Come on, Winna."

We left Jenny Lee squatted in the bean row and walked down our driveway. "I can't believe you'd even think about helping Jenny Lee break into old man Barr's garage," I said. "Mrs. Barr is nice, taking us to church and everything. If you got caught snooping around and stealing from them, it would be awful. You'd end up in juvie like Jenny Lee."

With annoyance in her voice, Veronica said, "When I heard what she wanted to do, the porch light came on before I could ditch her. Keep your trap shut about this."

"Don't worry. I'll be in trouble, too, and definitely don't want to upset Mama."

The living room light was on when we got home. I guess we weren't sneaky enough. There'd be a big uproar when we went into the house. Veronica grabbed my hand, and instead of crawling through the window, she pulled me down, and we sat on the front porch.

Puppy laid her head in my lap, and I whispered, "How are we getting out of this one?"

"Shut up and let me think." Veronica put her elbow on her knee and cupped her chin in her hand, and her scheming brain started ticking. After a minute, she stood and pointed toward me. "Okay, I'll do the talking." She opened the front door and softly called, "Here, Puppy," and our faithful, old companion eagerly followed her inside.

Mama sat on the couch in the living room that reeked of cigarette smoke. Veronica sat next to her and said, "Did all the racket wake you up, too?"

"Racket?" Mama ground her cigarette out in a dirty ashtray, furrowed her brows, and skeptically studied Veronica's face.

"A terrific growling and whining. Didn't you hear it?"

Mama gave Veronica a skeptical look. "No, I didn't."

I sat on the other side of Mama, and Puppy crawled up next to me. I scratched her soft ears, and she rewarded me with a dog-happy grin.

"Yeah." Veronica nodded. "We were afraid coyotes were beating up Puppy. Knowing you wouldn't want us to wake up Daddy, we went outside to check if she was okay. Took a while to find her, though. Whatever was out there probably ran off, but just in case, maybe she should sleep in the house."

Veronica was such a great liar I almost believed the story myself. Mama turned her gaze on me. To avoid an interrogation, I got up and called Puppy, and we went into my room. While I changed into my pajamas, she spryly hopped on my bed. I kept worrying until Veronica came in, winked, and patted Puppy, and then went to her room. After a while, Mama turned off the lights and plodded through the kitchen to the screened porch.

First thing in the morning, Puppy nosed my face and then hurried after me when I got out of bed to open the front door to let her outside. Plopping into a kitchen chair, I watched Mama frying bacon and waited to see if she was suspicious about last night.

She glanced at me but didn't mention anything about us roaming around in the middle of the night. She didn't look in too grouchy of a mood, either. Maybe this morning was a good time to ask Daddy about the saddle before something else happened to make her mad.

Veronica sat at the table with me and finger-combed strands of messy-morning hair behind her ears. "Smells good. Oh, man, am I hungry." She got up, retrieved a plate and a loaf of Wonder Bread from the cupboard, and started making toast.

"Make me some, too," I said.

She smiled. "I will if you do the dishes tonight."

Veronica was such a schemer. I shrugged. "Maybe."

Mama smeared jelly on a slice of toast and said, "Go tell your daddy it's time for breakfast."

I knocked on my parents' bedroom door and said, "Breakfast is ready, Daddy."

"Be there in a minute."

I waited outside his door. When he opened it, he looked down at me. His glasses sat crooked on his nose. Since we moved, he'd lost weight. His face was paler, thinner, and more wrinkled.

I pasted on my most meek expression and talked fast as I followed him into the kitchen. "Can I get a new saddle? The one we have is so big and heavy I can't lift it high enough to put it on Babyface, and a man down the road sells them, and he tried one on her that's perfect for me. Can I?"

He sat across the table from Mama, raised his eyebrows, and said, "I'll think about it."

After breakfast, to keep Mama in a good mood, I cleared the table and volunteered to wash the breakfast dishes. Then I went into Veronica's room and watched her burrow through the clothes she had tossed on the floor. She found the pair of jeans she wore last night and slipped them on.

I sat on her bed as she brushed her hair and bunched her dark mane into a ponytail. She outlined her lips with coral lipstick, kissed a tissue, leaving an orange lip print, and then dropped it on the dresser with three or four other smacked on tissues. She picked up a little red mascara box, opened it, and plucked out a tiny brush. She spit into her hand to moisten the brush and then rubbed it in the cake of black mascara. After brushing it onto her lashes, she admired herself in the mirror, turning her head from side to side.

Satisfied her makeup was perfect, she looked at me, studying my face the way a scientist would a laboratory specimen. "You need color. If you tried, you could be pretty." She dug through tubes of lipstick scattered on her dresser and chose one.

"Where'd you get all those lipsticks?" I asked.

She shrugged. "Jenny Lee."

"Did she steal them?"

Ignoring my question, Veronica grabbed my chin and intently stared at my face. "Hold your lips like this." She stretched her mouth into an odd half-smile.

I tried to mimic her, tightening my mouth into a wide grimace, and she smeared pink lipstick on my lips. "Now some mascara," she said and spat into the palm of her hand.

"Use my spit, instead," I said.

"Nope. Only *my* spit is touching *my* brush." After rubbing the mascara cake with the wet brush, she grabbed my chin again and tilted it up. "Don't blink," she said.

Worried she'd jab out my eye, I held as still as a statue. She finished brushing mascara on my lashes, then grasped my hand and pulled me to the mirror. Standing behind me, she peeked over my shoulder. "You look better, huh?"

I leaned closer to my reflection and fluttered my lashes. Was that me staring out from the mirror? With my pale lips transformed to bright pink and my blonde lashes now black, I did look different, like a girly-girl.

A knock at the front door startled me. I checked my new face before going to answer it. I jerked the door open as Ben's fist was ready to knock again. He stepped back and gawked at me. Was my makeup paying off, or did he think I looked like a clown?

Veronica quit fussing over herself and strolled into the living room. Ben's gaze wandered to her. "Uh, hi," he said. "Can't hunt for arrowheads this afternoon, so wanted to see if you could go now."

Ben waited on the porch while Veronica put on her shoes. Puppy and I ran up the hill ahead of them and went into the barn. The horses tromped in, and I watched and whispered to Chaos as she shyly nosed the hay I tossed into the manger.

Veronica and Ben came in, and they sat side by side on top of the haystack. Ben gazed up at the rough sawn rafters and said, "This old barn has been here a long time."

"Yeah," I said. "Betcha stage robbers buried loot here."

Veronica rolled her eyes. "Oh, sure. Gold worth millions is buried right here. Where should we start digging?"

What a witch Veronica was, trying to make me look stupid in front of Ben. "Why not," I said. "Stranger things have happened, ya know."

Chaos was startled when Trudy and Jenny Lee clomped into the barn. They climbed the haystack, and Jenny Lee crowded in next to Ben and Veronica. Trudy mutely stared gaga eyed at Ben, while Jenny Lee flipped back her hair, heaved her chest higher, and said, "What's doing?"

"We're going arrowhead hunting," Ben said. He stood, stretched his arms behind his back to show off his chest too. Then, he reached for the swinging rope, shimmied to the top, clutched the center beam, traversed it hand-over-hand, did a few chin ups, and then, to Veronica and Jenny Lee's applause, swung back and forth on the rope.

What a show-off. Guess I wasn't the only girl he liked to impress.

As I climbed onto the haystack, a piece of sharp straw gouged my finger. I sucked my finger to take the hurt away. Ben dropped down onto the stack and gave me an amused glance. Was my pink lipstick smeared?

"You know what?" he said. "If we find arrowheads, we should draw where we found them on a map. Put the location of this barn on it too."

I gazed at him. "Great idea," I said and fluttered my newly blackened lashes. "I can draw a map. It would be fun, but I'll need your help."

"I'll ask my brother to help you," Trudy piped in. "He's taking architecture in college." She peered at my face. "What happened to your eyes? Is that mascara? Mom says I'm too young to wear makeup."

I gritted my teeth and felt small enough to crawl into a mouse hole.

"Your brother's in college?" Veronica asked, her scheming boy-crazy brain working overtime.

"Yes. He will be a freshman this fall."

Jenny Lee's eyes widened and then turned cagey. "Oh? Really?"

Trudy's brother might create hot competition between Veronica and Jenny Lee. Maybe it would cool their friendship, and that'd be good. Jenny Lee probably stole those lipsticks and, sooner or later, she'd get Veronica into trouble. Then Mama would have a conniption fit and make my life miserable.

No longer the center of attention, Ben said, "Hey, where's that chalk rock pile?"

Everyone jumped off the stack. I led the way across the meadow and up the hill until we reached a mound of white rocks at the back of the pasture. "Looks like a burial place or an ancient altar, doesn't it?" I said.

"Farmers probably cleared the field and piled them there," Ben said.

Veronica climbed on top of the rocks, scanned the valley, and then raised her arms to the sky. "I'm the queen of the mountain."

All of us girls climbed on the rock pile too, stretched our arms to heaven, and repeated, "I'm queen of the mountain." Then we squealed with laughter.

Ben watched us with a stupid grin. Then he climbed up too and pounded his chest like Tarzan. "I'm king of the mountain."

His eyes lowered to mine. My lips trembled. I couldn't breathe right. An odd shiver swirled in the pit of my stomach. My heart did the jitterbug. Whoa, heart! The male-female animal-attraction thing had reared its horned head. My body had its own agenda. Me a moth and Ben the candle I'd like to fly into. I hated to be all fluttery about a boy who would probably want a cheerleader girlfriend. How stupid was that?

I forced my eyes away from his, took a deep breath, and pointed to the opposite side of the valley. "Let's go to Adventure Rock on top of the other hill."

We walked down to the meadow and then climbed up the steep hillside. The morning had grown hotter, and the sagebrush smelled spicy. By the time we reached the rocky ledge, I panted from the climb, not the boy.

I pointed to hollowed-out places on the ledge. "That must be where Indians ground acorns."

We all sat on the gravelly rock. Quail called to one another from the brushy valley below. Ben nodded. "It's beautiful here. If I were an Indian, this is where I'd sit and work. This should be on your map."

"This would be my favorite spot, too," Trudy said.

"If I were an Indian, I'd be Pocahontas," Jenny Lee said. She elbowed Veronica, and they giggled.

When we trekked back to the barnyard, Chaos was curious. She timidly watched while Ben showed us what Mr. Buck had taught him about organizing an archeological dig by drawing squares in the dirt to form a grid to search inside.

"So that's why those lines I saw were here," I said.

Ben nodded. "Winna, why don't you draw a map of this grid? As we search each square, if we find anything, you can write it down and keep a record like a real archeologist."

"Wait. Don't start looking yet. I'll run to the house and get a pencil and paper."

When I returned, I drew the grid map on the paper, then folded it and shoved it in my pocket. We each chose a square to search. Treasure hunting fascinated me, and I walked slowly and kept alert for triangular-shaped stones. It didn't take long before Veronica and Jenny Lee got bored and left. The rest of us kept searching but didn't find anything.

"If you guys are hungry, I'll make lunch," I said.

They both nodded. We headed for my house and went into the kitchen where Veronica was already making sandwiches. Daddy sat at the table with Jenny Lee, watching Veronica spread peanut butter and Mr. Barr's jelly on slices of bread.

"Winna, go look in the garage," Daddy said.

"Why? What have I done wrong now?"

I trudged into the garage and squealed. It was incredible. On top of a sawhorse was the saddle I had picked out. Daddy had bought the saddle with the flower pattern just for me.

Everyone came into the garage to see why I was squealing. Daddy's face wore a huge grin. I hugged him and laid my head against his chest. "It's the one I wanted. Thank you, Daddy."

Veronica gave me an evil look. "As usual, Daddy's little girl gets everything."

Chapter Fourteen
The Graveyard

"Want to go riding?" I asked Trudy. "Can't wait to try my new saddle."

With five families on our party line, anyone could overhear our telephone conversations. Privacy was impossible with snoopy neighbors. Mama thought the woman who lived at the dairy next door was a creepy voyeur and listener. I strained my ears for the familiar click or breathing that sometimes gave the old bag away.

"I'll ask." Trudy laid down the phone. While she and her mother chatted in the background, I heard the neighbor pick up the receiver. Trudy came back on the line and said, "I'll be over first thing."

"If I'm not at the house, I'll be up at the barn." Not wanting that snoopy neighbor to hear anything else, I quickly hung up.

The horses didn't come when I went into the barn, so I hiked to Adventure Rock and saw them down in the meadow. Gravel scrunched under my jeans as I slid down the hill's vertical trail on my rear end, whooping, "Ya-ha-hoo." At the bottom, I dusted off my backside and quietly approached Snafu. Raising her head, she glanced at me, but then, unconcerned, she continued to graze. Maybe today, she'd let me get near her baby.

Babyface ignored me too. Only little Chaos was curious. The spindly-legged filly's wispy mane stood upright along her short neck, and the stringy belly button cord had already shriveled and disappeared from her tummy.

To learn how to think like a horse and make friends with her, I squatted on my heels and waited. Little by little, the filly inched toward me, walked a few steps, then stopped and stared. I had to be patient and watch for her reactions the way I did with Babyface's ears. I didn't dare move, or I'd frighten her, or Snafu might get mad.

When close enough, Chaos stretched her neck to nuzzle me with her nose. Her milky breath was warm, and the whiskers sprinkled on her muzzle tickled as she sniffed my cheek and explored my face.

"Ouch!" I squealed and jumped up when she grabbed a mouthful of my hair and yanked. Startled, Chaos twirled and trotted to the safety of Snafu, who looked up, pinned her ears back like an angry lion, and then ignored me again.

Since I hadn't anticipated that Chaos would bite, I wasn't much good at thinking like a horse yet. Rubbing my sore scalp, I whispered, "Friends don't bite. Be a nice girl. I won't hurt you."

I squatted on my heels again, and the filly, still curious, crept toward me but didn't come as close this time. Tired of squatting, I stood. She shied away and didn't return.

Back inside the barn, I was welcomed by a silence that wrapped around me like a warm blanket. A hay hook shaped like Captain Hook's lost hand was anchored in a hay bale. I yanked it out and used it to twist the baling wire until it broke, and the bale popped open. Flakes of hay spewed apart like slices of a huge loaf of bread.

I tossed two flakes in the manger, and after a few minutes, the aroma of the freshly opened bale must have lured the horses into the barn. At first, Chaos suspiciously watched me, then sniffed and nibbled the fragrant hay.

While the mares ate, I ignored the filly, brushed Babyface, and told her my news. "Guess what? Daddy bought me a new saddle. Today you'll get to wear it. You probably won't like it, though."

Like Puppy, the horses would keep my secrets. They wouldn't yell or say I was stupid, only listen and crunch mouthfuls of hay in a calm, comforting rhythm.

After listening to me chitchat and watching me groom the mares, Chaos felt brave enough again to step closer. I whispered, "Want to be friends, little girl? Best friends?" I slowly raised my hand to reach out and stroke her fuzzy neck. This time, she didn't move. Instead, she let me gently scratch her forehead.

Then she became bold, snatched at the brush with her teeth, and flipped it out of my hand. When I stooped to pick it up, she shoved my butt with her nose and jumped back in surprise when I lost my balance and fell to my knees.

I scrambled to my feet, placed my hands on my hips, and said, "So you want to play? Well, being knocked down is not my idea of playing. Understand?"

To lure Chaos back, I grabbed a handful of hay, then heard a shout, "Winna."

I went out to the pasture gate, where Trudy was tying Blackie to a fence post. "Where's the new baby?" she asked.

"In the barn with her mama. I've been making friends with her, but Snafu doesn't know you, so we better be careful."

When we went into the barn, Snafu pinned her ears and herded Chaos outside, away from Trudy. We followed them out and trekked to Adventure Rock. We sat cross-legged on the gravelly rim to watch the filly frolic and kick.

Chaos stopped and watched us too but stayed close to her mother's side.

"The baby is *so* cute," Trudy said.

"As soon as Snafu settles down, Daddy and I will halter train the filly."

"Oh, that will be fun."

"I can hardly wait," I said. "Hunting for arrowheads was interesting, wasn't it?"

Trudy nodded and smiled. Ben would probably never want to kiss her. All those wires on her braces could slice up his lips. I was glad I didn't have to wear them. If I did, he'd never be interested in kissing me either, even with lipstick and black eyelashes.

Trudy grabbed my arm and squeezed. "Guess what! I told Mom about our arrowhead hunt, and she said there's an old graveyard nearby. It won't take long to ride there."

"Wow," I said. "A graveyard is even better than arrowheads. I could include it on my treasure map."

Blackie calmly waited on the other side of the gate. Trudy untied her and followed me as I led Babyface down to the garage where my new saddle sat in all its glory on the sawhorse. I placed a blanket on her back, but my new saddle was still difficult to lift even though it was lighter than the old one.

After tightening the cinch, I walked Babyface in circles and then rechecked it the way Joseph had done to make sure the saddle wouldn't slip off this time. With my thumb crammed in the corner of her lips, the new bit slid easily into her mouth. I tucked her ears neatly under the headstall and threw the reins over her neck. My ballerina toe-poke planted my foot into the stirrup, and I struggled up onto the saddle.

Once securely on top of Babyface's fat, round back, I glanced down to admire the flower imprinted on the saddle horn. Probably full of envy, Trudy hadn't said a peep about my new saddle.

"Lead the way," I said and tracked behind Blackie. I only had to swat Babyface's rump once with the reins to push her along when she tried to snatch a mouthful of grass. My new saddle's polished leather squeaked in rhythm with her steps. I felt like a real cowgirl.

Along the way, Trudy saw a neighbor that she knew digging into the side of a hill in his front yard. We rode over to find out what he was doing.

"Hi, Mr. Earl," Trudy said. "Why are you digging?"

He stopped working and said, "Hello, you two." He gazed down at the hole. "It's going to be an A-bomb shelter. This mountain is solid chalk rock. It's a perfect place for one."

"A-bomb shelter?" I said.

"If the Russians drop a bomb on us, I'm going to be ready." Mr. Earl stared into the distance and leaned on his shovel. "I fought in World War II. After we dropped Fat Man and Little Boy on Japan, I thought I wouldn't have to worry about war anymore. I thought those atomic bombs would teach everyone a lesson."

He pulled a hanky from his back pocket and wiped his brow. "But no! The Russians stole our secrets about building an atomic bomb. Now we have to worry about being blown to smithereens. A cold war, they call it. Well, I'm not waiting for the cold war to turn hot. I'm getting ready."

Trudy nodded. "Dad said being so close to the Air Force base makes us a target."

"Sure does," Mr. Earl said. He stooped to hoist a rock from the pile of rubble he had loosened with his pick and grunted from the effort. He straightened, rubbed his back, and nodded. "Uncle Sam taught me how to dig foxholes. That'll come in handy now. They have a bomb shelter in town, but it's too far away if they drop the big one. Besides, in a community shelter, we'd be crowded together like a cage full of rats."

"You were a soldier in the war?" I asked. With his narrow, wrinkled face and stuck out ears, Mr. Earl wasn't young and handsome like soldiers in the movies.

"Sure was. Saw a lot of action in World War II. The Battle of the Bulge. I don't want to re-live that one. It was rough." He mopped his forehead again and then stuck the handkerchief back into his pocket. "Now I gotta worry about the big mushroom cloud hanging over all our heads."

Mr. Earl gazed at his heavy, laced boots and cleared his throat. "Well, I better get back to work. Have a good ride." He turned, swung the pick, and it hit the ground with a thud.

It seemed it was as difficult for countries to make friends as it was for me. Trusting people with my secrets would be a mistake. Later, they could be used as ammunition against me—the way Russia did with our atomic bomb secrets.

After we'd ridden down the road, I said, "Gads, won't countries ever be friendly? Don't you love knowing we could be blown up, and the end of the world could happen any minute? We should find out where the town's bomb shelter is."

"We should build a bomb shelter," Trudy said.

"Does your dad know how?"

Trudy looked at me. "I suppose. He's an engineer. Except, he was in the Air Force. I don't think he dug foxholes."

"We'd need to build a huge bomb shelter," I said. "One big enough for the horses too. I couldn't stand it if the horses weren't safe. It would get pretty stinky, though, like Noah's Ark. I wonder how long we'd have to stay in it. The horses wouldn't like it."

Trudy laughed. "It would stay nice and warm in there with all of us and the horses too. We wouldn't need a heater, but we'd need something to get rid of the smell."

"Maybe a smell vacuum," I said and then giggled. "We'd get rich if we invented a smell vacuum cleaner for bomb shelters."

We came to the Arroyo Viejo Creek, the same one flowing through the town. Trudy urged Blackie to step onto a wooden bridge. It was barely wide enough for two people to pass each other, and the mare refused. Crowding Babyface in front of them, I kicked her, but she refused too. Turning the horses, we rode along the creek bank until we found a shallow place where the water was only up to our horse's knees as they splashed across.

Riding on a farm road that cut between broccoli fields, an unpleasant aroma wafted by my nose. "Phew! These vegetable fields are so pretty but so stinky!"

Trudy made me laugh when she mushed up her face and pinched her nose with her fingers.

Coming to a wire gate, she got off Blackie to open it. Cows didn't look up from grazing as we passed by to reach a gigantic oak tree that shaded the old graveyard. We tied the horses and went to read the tombstones.

With no fence to protect the graveyard, wandering cows had toppled and haphazardly strewn marble tombstones and split the wooden grave markers into pieces. I searched through the dead weeds under the oak for headstones and tried to patch the wooden markers together. "Look," I said. "These markers are like a jigsaw puzzle. This piece matches that one. Can't read the names and dates on the old wooden ones but can still read the marble ones."

"Looks like most of the people buried were children," Trudy said.

I bent to peer at the names more closely. "I should draw a map of this graveyard. If I don't, the tombstones might disappear, and no one will know people are buried here."

I tripped over a mound of dirt piled up by squirrels. My feet sunk in the damp, musky earth as if graves wanted to claim me. I shuttered. "Let's go. It's creepy here."

Trudy hugged herself and nodded.

The horses dozed in the shade. We woke them up, untied them, and silently rode toward home. It seemed ghosts followed us. All those dead people with their scattered tombstones made me sad. Did it even matter who they were or whether they'd lived? Maybe being an archeologist wasn't such a great idea. It wasn't like treasure hunting. A circus was a happier place to work than a spooky graveyard full of dead peoples' bones.

With head lowered, Babyface lagged after Blackie. Trudy turned and hollered, "Yesterday, I watched Ben play baseball."

I kicked Babyface to catch up. "Oh? You saw Ben?" So, now I knew where he was yesterday afternoon. This trying to get a boyfriend thing was becoming more complicated. I wanted to be friends with Trudy, but she like Ben, too. He was so cute. Who wouldn't have a crush on him?

Trudy grinned. "My dad helps coach Ben's team. We'll be going to all his games. Ben's a great pitcher. With him playing, the team has a good chance to win the championship."

My heart dropped into my stomach, leaving a bitter taste in my mouth. Oh, great! Trudy would be at Ben's games. Annoyed, when we came to the creek, I kicked Babyface hard, and she took a few cautious steps onto the narrow bridge.

It began to sway.

Then it stopped, and I hauled on the reins to make her back up.

Babyface froze and wouldn't budge.

Clinging to the saddle horn, I glanced over the edge. The creek was only a few feet below. Not too far, but I was scared Babyface might fall.

Terrified of a bridge collapse, I gulped for a breath. My heart raced at high speed, and I couldn't think. Staring straight ahead, I tried to will my brain to work. *Don't panic, don't look down,* spun around in my mind.

Before I figured out what to do, Babyface did. She slowly crept back. The bridge swayed. She stopped. When the bridge stopped swaying, she took another tiny step. The bridge swayed again. She stopped, then stepped, then stopped, then stepped until she'd backed off the bridge and onto the creek bank.

I could breathe again.

Trudy's eyes bulged out like two blue olives. "For a minute, I was sure Babyface would jump off," she said.

Holding my reins with one shaky hand, I licked my dry lips and swallowed what felt like a cotton ball stuck in my throat. Oh, man, was I stupid or what? If I asked Babyface to do dumb things like getting on a wobbly bridge, she'd never trust me. I took a deep breath, leaned against her golden neck and stroked her. My voice quivered when I said, "Babyface is smart, isn't she? Thank you, girl. You're such a good horse."

Crossing the creek at the shallow spot, halfway across, we stopped to let the horses drink.

Babyface splashed with her front hoof, which was fun until, like a flash, she dropped to her knees.

"Stop! Stop!" I screamed.

As she lay down on her side, I kicked my feet out of the stirrups. My right foot touched the gravelly creek bed, and I managed to scramble off and out of the way as she tried to roll in the icy water. Avoiding Babyface's thrashing hoofs, I frantically clung onto the reins and held her head up to prevent her from completely rolling over on my new saddle.

I tugged on the reins, and with a loud grunt, Babyface hauled herself up. Once standing, she shook and splattered water everywhere, but mostly on me. I couldn't believe it. She hated getting a bath. Now she was a water lover.

As I led Babyface up to the creek bank, Trudy laughed and held her stomach as if hearing the funniest joke ever. Between giggles, she asked, "Are you okay?"

"It's not funny! My new saddle is wet and could have been crushed. I'm sopping wet and cold, but I'm okay. No thanks to you." I was so angry my ears were probably steaming. What kind of friend laughed when you almost got hurt and your new saddle was almost ruined?

"I'm sorry, but the look on your face was just so funny."

With a smirky grin, Trudy watched me twist and squeeze water from my shirttail. Before I could climb back in the saddle, Babyface reached down to gobble grass. Jerking on the reins, I hollered, "No snacks. You're bad and a pig, too. I'll never let you get a drink from the creek again. You deserve a spanking." After counting to ten, then twenty, I gathered my reins and my temper, found a high place to mount, and scaled back up onto my wet saddle.

I didn't speak a word on the way home. We rode by the still digging Mr. Earl, and Trudy gaily waved at him, but she must have known I was furious. At my driveway, she smiled sweetly and said, "Bye-bye," then turned Blackie toward home.

I didn't acknowledge her good-bye. At the garage, I unsaddled and checked my saddle over. It was wet, but it didn't look scratched or damaged. Except it might take forever to dry out and lose its damp smell. I was glad to have avoided a catastrophe but was still perturbed. It was my fault she'd rolled in the creek. I needed to learn how to think like a horse.

At the barn, I slipped Babyface's halter off. Snafu and Chaos came in, and the mares sniffed noses and squealed a greeting. Chaos wandered over, investigated the halter I still had in my hand, then grabbed it with her teeth.

"Do you want to wear a halter, little girl?"

If I asked Ben to help me train her, we'd spend time alone. It would be way better than watching him play baseball, and Daddy would be surprised if I taught Chaos how to lead.

Chapter Fifteen
At the Movies

Sundays, we usually went to church, but I loved going to the movie theater on Saturdays. The movies started at noon, with a double feature, cartoons, and best of all, no adults. It was heavenly sitting in the dark, eating a Heath Bar, and watching movies, especially the ones with cowboys galloping horses and doing wild stunts.

I didn't have enough nerve to ask Ben to go with me. If I hadn't still been stewed at Trudy, I would have invited her. Veronica was meeting Jenny Lee and wouldn't let me sit with them. They'd probably sit with boys. That was what Veronica liked about going to the movies: boys.

Veronica parked the Chevy, and when we got out, she looked around to see if anyone noticed her. The billboard over the theater said, "Audie Murphy Day." Mama had given us each a dollar. We paid for our tickets, and when we got into the lobby, the buttery smell of fresh popcorn filled my nostrils. Tempted by colorful boxes of candy inside the glass counter, I bought some Milk Duds, then went into the theater. The lights were dim, and tiny lights along the aisle illuminated the red carpet to help me find a seat.

Cartoons would play first, then a war movie, *To Hell and Back*, starring Audie Murphy and based on his life story. Audie was a real WWII hero and cute too. The battles seemed so real in war movies. Soldiers fought hand to hand, throwing grenades, tromping through snow, rain, and mud, shooting at tanks or airplanes during dive-bomb attacks.

After I'd sat on the edge of my seat watching Audie face horrible dangers, there would be an intermission, and then the second feature would be another one of his movies, but it would be a western. Of course, he'd be the hero.

When the cartoons started, Veronica came to where I sat and said, "Come sit with me."

Veronica said her friends thought I was a pest and never invited me to sit with her. So why did she ask me? I was suspicious but followed her to the back row where kids sat so they could make out.

I tried not to stumble into someone's lap as we squeezed by people to an empty seat. Veronica pointed at it, indicating I should sit there, and said to the boy in the next seat, "Harold, this is my sister, Winna."

"Hi," he said.

Then Veronica sat in the seat on the other side of Harold, next to another boy.

Oh, great! Now I got it. Jenny Lee didn't show up, so I was supposed to fill in for her with this guy. Tense as a cricket ready to hop, I sat next to him.

It was nerve-racking sitting with a boy, especially with my silly sister giggling next to me. I glanced over at Harold. The light from the screen flickered on his face. I couldn't tell what he looked like, which was good because he couldn't see my face either.

Staring straight ahead at the huge screen, I tried to concentrate on the movie. A war was happening in front of my eyes. The German army threatened to kill one of my favorite movie stars. He could be shot any minute.

Inch-by-inch Harold's arm crept along the back of my seat. I leaned forward, hoping he would get the hint. The idiot leaned forward, too. I got a whiff of his Sin-Sin gum breath as he twisted around to plant a kiss on me.

I jerked back to avoid his lips. Gads, what nerve! I didn't even know him. We'd never even said, "Hi," before.

It made me so mad I wanted to scream. I could hardly breathe and sat stiff as a stone. Then his arm tried to slither around my shoulders again. What a jerk. He probably thought I was gulping for breath because I was hot for him.

What should I do? I'd die of embarrassment if I didn't escape. I jumped up, and his arm fell with a whack. I stepped on toes as I hurriedly squeezed back along the row to the aisle. In the cover of darkness, I found an empty seat on the other side of the theater.

Now, I couldn't enjoy the movie. I felt stupid. It was all Veronica's fault. She'd better never expect me to fill in for Jenny Lee again. I was mad enough to spit.

I'd pretty much calmed down when the intermission lights went on for trips to the snack bar. Two rows ahead, a boy that looked like Ben sat with a girl. She had blonde hair and a ponytail like Trudy's. Could it be Ben? I couldn't tell for sure because all I could see was the back of their heads.

The boy left his seat to go to the lobby. I scrunched down as he walked by. It was Ben. The lights dimmed, and the movie began before he returned with two bags of popcorn and offered one to the girl. I tried to focus on the movie but mostly spied on Ben and *her*. The only good thing was they weren't kissing and giggling like Veronica and her boyfriend.

My stomach churned, and the Milk Duds I'd eaten tasted sour in my mouth. It seemed hours and hours passed before the movie ended, and the screen went blank. I scrunched down again when Ben and the girl stood to leave. When they strolled by, I had to peek.

It was who I'd imagined, Trudy.

It took all my will power to stop myself from turning and gawking as they walked up the aisle. I was glad they didn't notice me ducking behind the seat. If they had, I would have looked like a fool. I waited until everyone left the theater before going to the lobby, hoping they wouldn't be there.

They weren't, but in a huff, Veronica was.

She peered at me with a wicked glare. "Thanks for jumping up and making a scene. Everyone looked. Never speak to me again. Never!"

Crossing my arms over my chest, I glared back and said, "I didn't appreciate being stuck with Harold. It was embarrassing. I definitely didn't want to be kissed by him with his hot, stinky breath. If he's Jenny Lee's boyfriend, he's a big creep trying to kiss me. Why do all that kissing anyway? You can't watch the movie."

Before I could go to the candy counter and buy gum to get the bitter taste out of my mouth, Veronica grabbed my wrist and turned me to face her. "Practice, that's why. You've got to practice."

"Practice for what?" I said and twisted my wrist from her grasp.

"To be a great kisser, you've got to practice, or you won't learn how. Practice makes perfect." Veronica laughed at her stupid joke. "You'll never be popular if you don't have a boyfriend, and never have a boyfriend if you're not a good kisser."

I shook my head. "I don't want to be a good kisser. Besides, I thought you were supposed to like the boy you kiss. I don't even know Harold, and I don't like him!"

"You're so stupid. You'd be lucky to be kissed by him."

I shrugged. "Lucky me."

Was being a good kisser why Veronica was popular and always had a boyfriend? If it took practice to become great at kissing, I wanted to practice with the boy who'd been sitting in the theater with my supposed friend, Trudy. My first kiss shouldn't happen with some stupid boy I didn't even like and didn't even know.

My first kiss should be the way it was in the movies. Ben would hold my hand with a longing look in his eyes. Slowly, he'd lean toward me with his full lips pursed a bit. Irresistibly drawn toward them, my racing heart would jump, my spine tingle. Our feelings would overtake us. Our lips would lightly touch. His would taste like vanilla.

If Ben and I ever kissed, I wanted to impress him with a perfect one. He'd forget about other girls and fall crazily, madly in love with me. Maybe Veronica was right, and I should have ignored how icky Harold was and let him give me a practice kiss.

Veronica glared at me and then walked outside, digging in her purse for the car keys. We sat in silence all the way home. When we got there, I read a note stuck on the refrigerator: *We've gone to the hospital. Warm up the goulash in the icebox for dinner. Veronica's in charge until I get home.*

"Gads," I said. "Daddy must be sick."

"Probably his diabetes is acting up," Veronica said after she'd read the note too.

While Veronica warmed the goulash, I set the table. The big dinette looked bare with only two plates. We sat down but didn't feel like eating. After picking through the noodles in the goulash, I turned on the radio, and the announcer said, "In case of emergency, tune to 640 or 1240 on your radio dial."

In a national emergency, we were supposed to tune in civil defense radio stations to find out what to do. At school, we practiced ducking under our desks in case the Russians tried to blow us up with an A-bomb. Or was it the Chinese? Now Daddy might be sick. I was worried but tuning in a radio station wouldn't help. I couldn't do anything except feel afraid.

I closed my eyes and whispered, "Please, please, God, help Daddy. I know there are lots of big problems in the world, but I need him to be okay."

My eyes were still shut when Veronica said in her bossiest voice, "I made dinner, so you'll wash the dishes."

My lids sprung open. "All you did was warm up leftovers."

With her hands on her hips, Veronica squawked, "Shut up, Winna. Or is it Whiney? No comments from the peanut gallery."

"You shut up."

"No, you shut up. Mama left me in charge. It's your turn, and that's that because I said so. Period."

I stood and faced Veronica. "You're not my boss."

She shoved her nose close to my face. "Tonight I am."

What a conniver. Veronica tried to use me at the movies and now thought she'd take advantage because Mama wasn't here. Almost every night we argued over whose turn it was to do the dishes, but Mama was usually our referee.

I was stressed and so ticked off my head buzzed. Tonight wasn't the night to mess with me.

Without thinking, I slapped her.

Veronica was quick. She grabbed my hair, and we yelled insults, slapped and kicked, and wrestled to the floor.

We were on the floor scratching and screaming when Mama came into the kitchen and yelled, "Stop. Stop. Are you girls crazy? Can't I trust you to get along without me?"

We stopped wrestling and got up off the floor before Mama got the broom.

Still angry, I yelled one last insult.

Mama scowled. Her shoulders sagged as she plopped down on a kitchen chair. Leaning her elbows on the table, she pressed her palms against her eyes, sighed, and then burst out crying.

I'd never seen Mama cry like this before. Her shoulders heaved up and down between huge sobs and gulps of air.

I felt terrible and guilty. "Mama, I'm sorry." I bit my lip to keep from crying too. My arms wrapped around her, I rested my head against her shoulder and smelled whiskey.

"Yeah, we won't argue anymore," Veronica said, her face still an angry red.

"We'll be good," I agreed.

Minutes crept by while Mama wept. Veronica and I sat at the table and stared at the floor, unable to look at each other or her.

"Daddy fell and hit his head," Mama finally said when she stopped crying. "When I left the hospital, he was asleep."

She looked at us with puffy red and weary eyes. "The doctors say his brain is hemorrhaging. They don't know if he'll wake up." A sob escaped from her throat. "What will we do without him?"

"I've been praying, Mama," I said. "God will help Daddy." Looking into her sad eyes, I didn't know what else to say.

"We better count on the doctors, not God," Veronica said. "God's not worried about us."

Why did Veronica have to say a mean thing like that? God did care about Daddy. He had to care. Who else could help now? I would pray harder than ever. I was sure Mama was praying. She'd feel better knowing I was too.

"Daddy isn't young and as strong as he used to be." Mama sighed. "I'll be at the hospital a lot and don't want to come home to any more fighting like I saw tonight. You have to grow up and be more responsible. After all, you're not girls anymore."

"Let's make a schedule and keep track of the chores," I said. "Then we'll know who washed the dishes last."

"I'll make up the schedule," Veronica said.

"No," I said. "Mama should."

"Tomorrow," she said. "I'll write everything down. While I'm at the hospital, I won't be able to do much around the house. I'll need you girls to help. Now, I'm going to bed. I'm worn out."

Mama got up and walked out the back door to her empty room.

Later, barefoot and in my pajamas, I knocked on her door.

No answer.

The door wasn't locked, so I went in.

I climbed into bed next to Mama.

Her pillow muffled sobs.

I snuggled against her back and tightly hugged her. "Everything will be all right, Mama. I love you."

Chapter Sixteen
Sissies

Something chased me. I ran faster and faster until I came to a wall impossible to climb. The scary dream woke me. Trembling, I looked outside at an overcast sky as gray as I felt.

I was alone in bed, and it was cold. I huddled in the blankets and stared at the ceiling awhile before climbing out from under the covers. I went into the kitchen where Mama sat at the table rummaging through her purse.

"What's going on?" I asked.

"I'm going to the hospital," she said.

"Me too."

"Not today. Tomorrow I'll take you and Veronica. Your daddy will be stronger then."

The phone's shrill ring interrupted my argument when Mama rushed to answer it. "Hello. Yes, thank you. I'm going over this morning." Her lips tightened as she listened. "Trudy wants to talk to you." She handed me the phone.

Still annoyed about Trudy being at the movies with Ben, I wasn't in the mood to talk to her, but took the phone and politely said, "Hello."

"Sorry about your dad."

My voice trembled when I asked, "How do you know about Daddy?"

"Mom was working at the hospital yesterday when your mother brought him into the emergency room. Are you going to the hospital?"

"Not until tomorrow when my dad's stronger."

"Would you like to come over?"

I hesitated a moment but couldn't stop from saying, "You honestly want me to? I saw you at the movies with Ben. Now that he's your boyfriend, don't you want to spend time with him instead?"

"I didn't see you," Trudy said. "I saw Ben and his little sister there, and she invited me to sit with them. He isn't my boyfriend. Even if he were, I'd never break up our friendship over a boy."

She claimed we were friends, but she didn't know me. I wasn't sure I believed her anyway. It was nice that she invited me to her house, but I wasn't in the mood to be friendly today. Trying to erase annoyance from my voice, I said, "Don't know about coming over. I'll call when I find out what's happening. Talk to you later." Without waiting for a reply, I hung up.

Pulling on a gray jacket, Mama came into the living room. With her brow twisted in a worried knot, she said, "Might not be back until 4:00 or 5:00. I'll call if it's later."

Veronica came in, and Mama gave her a list of chores, frowned, and said, "Can you two please stay out of trouble while I'm gone?"

Veronica brushed back a lock of hair still tangled from last night's sleep. "Sure, Mama. Don't worry. We'll be good."

About half an hour after Mama left, Jenny Lee came over. I almost didn't recognize her. Her way-over-permed frizzy hair was now coal-black. With eyebrows penciled black and wearing blood-red lipstick, she looked weird, like a witch or the bride of Frankenstein. She gave me the heebie-jeebies.

"Hi," she said and then sauntered after Veronica.

They went into my sister's bedroom and shut the door. Getting on my knees, I pressed my ear against it and heard Jenny Lee say, "Grandma said your dad's in the hospital."

I peeked through the keyhole. Jenny Lee stood behind Veronica, who sat at her vanity. They stared at each other in the mirror.

Good, Jenny Lee wasn't a vampire. I could see her reflection.

Veronica nodded, and her shoulders drooped. "He had a serious accident."

Jenny Lee picked up a comb and parted my sister's hair, first on one side, then the other, as if deciding which way it looked best.

Ha, as if she would know.

Parting my sister's hair down the center, Jenny Lee began braiding it into a French braid. When she finished, Veronica held a hand mirror up and turned to see the back of her hair. Satisfied how great it looked, she got up, and they moved out of my view.

What were they doing? I scooted around to rearrange my eyeball to get a better view through the keyhole, and my knee accidentally thumped against the door.

"What's that?" Jenny Lee asked.

Afraid they'd open the door and find me on my knees, I quickly stood and knocked. Knowing it was probably me, they didn't answer. I opened the door anyway. Sitting side by side on the floor with their backs against the bed, they glanced up from a magazine when I came in.

I tried to act casual as if I hadn't been spying. "Uh, want to go to the barn and swing on the hangman's rope?"

They looked at each other. Veronica shrugged, and Jenny Lee said, "Yeah. It'd be fun. Gotta get something first. I'll meet you up there."

After she left, I inspected Veronica's hairdo. "Your braid looks nice."

Veronica grinned and patted her hair. "Yeah, Jenny Lee learned how to do all kinds of braids in juvie. She's thinking about becoming a beautician too."

"Yeah," I said. "I bet she learned a lot of interesting things in there. Did she swipe another magazine for you?"

Veronica shrugged. "I don't ask."

Why would she want a dropout and a thief like Jenny Lee for a friend? Especially now with Daddy so sick, Mama would be upset if she found out Jenny Lee swiped magazines and gave them to Veronica.

My sister quit admiring herself in the mirror, found a pair of jeans, and slipped them on. Puppy followed us up to the barn and sat on top of the haystack to watch while we took turns swinging on the hangman's rope.

Jenny Lee showed up, pulled a gallon jug out of a grocery bag, and held it up for us to see. Veronica stopped swinging, landed on the haystack, and gave me the rope. Before taking my turn, I pointed at Jenny Lee's jug of yellow liquid. "What's in the bottle?"

"Try some." Holding the gallon jug by its neck, she offered it to me.

It looked like the big bottle of kerosene Daddy said never to touch. I shook my head. "It isn't labeled. Is it safe to drink?"

"Yeah. Is it?" Veronica asked.

"It's a bottle of wine I lifted from old man Barr's garage," Jenny Lee said. "It makes you feel good." She twisted off the cap, tipped the bottle, and took a big swig. "See, it's not poison."

Veronica jumped down off the haystack, took the bottle, sniffed it, and offered it up to me. "You first, Winna."

"Why should I be first? You try it."

Veronica shrugged, hoisted the heavy bottle to her lips, took a small sip, and stuck out her tongue. "Ugh, it tastes like vinegar." She lifted the bottle and offered it to me again. "Your turn."

No way was she going to show me up. I let go of the rope, climbed down, grasped the large jug with both hands and tasted it. "Yuck. It's horrible. If it's not poison, it sure tastes like it." I wiped my tongue on my sleeve to erase the sour tang.

"What a sissy," Jenny Lee said. "Besides, you don't drink wine for the taste." She took the bottle and gulped a big, sour mouthful, then gave it back to Veronica.

My sister held her breath, took a sip, and tried to pass the jug back to me. I shook my head. How could Mama drink stuff that tasted this bad?

Jenny Lee took the bottle and sat. She leaned back against a hay bale, took a swallow, and then said, "You want a smoke?" She looked at me. "Suppose you're too sissy." She stuck a cigarette between her red lips, lit it, took a deep drag, and then blew smoke rings.

Jenny Lee puffed more rings and then handed the cigarette to my sister, who inhaled and started coughing.

While Veronica hacked, Trudy wandered into the barn. "What are you guys doing?"

Jenny Lee glared at her. "What do you think? A little smoke, a little wine makes this woman feel fine."

Trudy stared at the wine jug wedged between Jenny Lee's knees, then at the cigarette gripped between Veronica's fingers. "You're not supposed to smoke. Where'd you get cigarettes?"

"Grownups always say we're not supposed to do something," Jenny Lee said, "and then they do it. If it's so bad, why do they smoke?"

"It's wrong to smoke until you're eighteen and old enough to buy cigarettes legally. Until then, you shouldn't." Trudy clamped her lips and stared at me. "You're not smoking, are you, Winna?"

I didn't want to smoke, but Trudy annoyed me with her I'm-so-perfect act. Besides, in the movies, they smoked with long black cigarette holders and always looked glamorous. "Give me the cigarette," I said. "It can't hurt to try a puff. It won't kill me."

Veronica handed it to me, and I took a big drag like Jenny Lee. Gads, was I sorry. Choking and coughing, I leaned against the haystack, dizzy. I hated to admit it, but Trudy was right. This wasn't anything like the movies.

"Ha, hee, ha," Jenny Lee laughed like a donkey.

Trudy crossed her arms over her chest. "Well, I'm going home. Winna, if you want to go riding, call me."

Jenny Lee jabbed her finger toward Trudy. "Don't run home and tell Mommy."

With hands clamped on her hips, Trudy drew her lips back in a snarl. Her braces could cause major damage to Jenny Lee's poking finger.

"I'm not a tattletale. See you later, Winna," Trudy said and strode out of the barn.

Jenny Lee smirked. "Good riddance to bad rubbish." She snatched the cigarette from between my fingers and accidentally dropped it in the loose hay scattered on the barn floor.

Before a flame could flicker into a blaze, I leaped to crush out the cigarette and stomp the small flare-up. Puppy frantically barked when I started digging and throwing dirt on the smoldering straw. She started digging too. So did my sister and Jenny Lee.

After we had piled dirt into a small mound, I stopped digging and screamed at Jenny Lee, "You idiot. You could have burned the barn down."

Mad enough to spit, I continued to kick around the loose hay in search of smoldering straw to squelch any possibility of a fire.

"Quit worrying, sissy," Jenny Lee said. "Nothing caught on fire."

"Luckily, it didn't," I said.

Jenny Lee would be easy to hate. How could Veronica like her? To make friends, you've got to be a friend, but some people weren't good friend material. At least goody-two-shoes Trudy wasn't a juvenile delinquent and didn't try to act tough, steal, or get in a fight over a can of beer.

Still dizzy and a bit nauseous, I sat down, cupped my forehead in my hands, and hoped the feeling would pass. Puppy stopped barking, crowded against me, and licked my chin.

"Come here, Winna," Veronica said. "Let's see who's a sissy."

I looked up from my misery. The horses had heard the commotion and had come into the barn, expecting hay. Veronica stood at Babyface's left shoulder on the other side of the partition. My sister's face was smudged with dirt. Mine probably was too. I took a deep breath to clear my head and examined my singed fingers with their black, dirty nails.

"Hurry up," Veronica said and aimed a determined stare at me when I hesitated.

What kind of nutty thing did my sister plan to do? I grasped a thick board on the partition, climbed over it, and stood on the manger's wooden railing.

Veronica led Babyface over to stand alongside me and said, "Get on."

It seemed like a stupid idea. Except, Jenny Lee was watching, and I didn't want to look chicken. My knees quivered as I clutched Babyface's mane, laid my stomach on top of her back, then swung my right leg over to the other side and sat upright.

Babyface nosed my foot, splattered me with a sneeze, and quietly stood there until Veronica swung up behind me. Grasping my waist, my sister yelled, "Hang on," and kicked hard.

Without a bridle or saddle, Babyface galloped wildly out of the barn. Excited by her sudden exit, Snafu and Chaos rushed madly behind her down the steep trail.

I leaned forward and clung to Babyface's neck like a scared chimpanzee. Behind me, Veronica hugged my waist as we raced down the trail into the valley. I was amazed we stayed on when, in true Babyface fashion, the mare halted, then abruptly spun and galloped back up the trail toward the barn.

Jenny Lee's mouth dropped open when the galloping horses met her hiking down the trail. "Stampede," I yelled, and she jumped off the path.

The horses rushed into the barn. "What a ride." Veronica laughed as she nimbly jumped off.

Gulping for air, I grasped the mare's blonde mane and carefully slid down. "Yeah, that's for sure." Then a bit of exhilaration replaced some of my shakes. "Guess we showed Jenny Lee."

In a few minutes, an out-of-breath Jenny Lee trudged into the barn. "Let me ride her."

We stepped back, and she grabbed Babyface's mane, flung her leg high, but couldn't swing up. She kept trying, but the annoyed mare wouldn't stand still.

Veronica haltered Babyface and led her to the water trough. We washed our filthy hands and faces, but my pitiful fingernails still looked nasty.

My sister shoved Babyface over so Jenny Lee could climb on. Once settled upon her back, Jenny Lee said to Veronica, "Get on behind me."

Veronica shook her head and gave Jenny Lee the lead rope for a rein. She shrugged and then kicked the mare into a trot. Laughing and bouncing, she clutched the thick mane. Of course, Babyface headed straight for the barn. Jenny Lee barely ducked her head in time as they trotted through the barn door.

We followed them in. Jenny Lee lay stretched on top of Babyface's fat back. Stroking the mare's silken neck, she said, "Her hair is so soft, and I can feel her breathe."

Puppy and I climbed up on the haystack. I noticed the wine jug almost hidden by loose straw and picked it up. "Look, nasty junk is floating in this stuff. It tastes so awful. How can you drink it?"

Jenny Lee sat upright. "It's pieces of fruit old man Barr didn't filter out. It tastes bad, but it's fun to drink. It makes me feel good."

Jenny Lee was wrong. Mama wasn't happy when she drank. "If alcohol makes people feel good," I said, "then why do they act so unhappy when they drink it?"

Jenny Lee shrugged and laughed. Sliding off, she combed her fingers through Babyface's mane. "Riding horseback is the most fun ever. I love your horse. Wish I had one."

"Yeah, riding Babyface *is* the most fun ever," I said. Jenny Lee was a sad case. Maybe owning a horse would help change things in her lousy life.

Veronica grasped the hangman's rope, and we took turns swinging again. After a while, bored, they walked down to the house with Jenny Lee toting her jug.

Worried Mama might find out we'd almost burned down the barn, I smoothed out the dirt pile to get rid of any evidence and checked again for smoldering hay.

Once satisfied that the barn was safe and no straw looked burned, I decided to brush Babyface. "Daddy's sick," I told her.

Overwhelmed by sadness, I leaned against her shoulder. An ache swelled in my chest, and tears welled up. I cleared my throat and prayed, "Please, God, don't let Daddy die!"

Squeezing my eyes tight, I smothered my wet face against her warm neck and sniffled the tears trickling into my nose. Daddy had to get well.

Except, maybe Veronica was right. God doesn't listen to me.

After all, He'd hardly ever answered my prayers. Perhaps this time, I wouldn't get what I wanted either.

I suppose if God answered every prayer, no one would get sick or die. We'd all live forever.

Chapter Seventeen
The Visit

When I got back to the house, Mama was in the kitchen washing green beans, getting them ready to cook. "Help me string these beans, Winna," she said.

After stringing and snapping the beans in half, we threw them into a large pot. Mama added salt pork, filled the pot with water, and then turned on the stove's burner to bring everything to a boil.

Then Mama sat across the table from me. "I know you want to see your daddy, so you and Veronica can go to the hospital with me tomorrow." She took my hand and looked into my eyes. "I'm sure he'll recover, but don't be surprised when you see him. He's sick and doesn't look like himself. Right now, he needs help breathing, and needles are stuck in his arms."

It didn't sound as if Daddy was getting better. Did I want to see him? How bad did he look? I was afraid to even think about losing him. Mama needed him as much as Veronica and I did. What would happen if he died? Who would take care of us?

"Okay," I said and stared at the table, unable to look at Mama. If my eyes reflected my fear, she could see how afraid I was.

As we got ready to go to the hospital the next morning, Mama counted the money in her wallet. Then she said, "Hurry up. Veronica, you drive. I'm too nervous."

Had she been drinking this morning?

Veronica slid behind the Chevy's steering wheel, and I climbed in the back seat. On the road to the hospital, we passed the county garbage dump. A man lived at the dump in a shack and kept the trash constantly burning. I'd hate living where it stunk, and smoke always wafted up from the ground. That was what hell must be like, stinky and hot.

We arrived at the huge white hospital that took up the whole block. It wasn't visiting hours yet, and hardly any cars were parked along the street. Veronica easily found a space by the front entrance. Three stories of windows stared down at us as we climbed the steps. In the green-carpeted lobby, a few people sat in the stiff brown chairs of the waiting room.

At the front desk, a nurse looked up when Mama asked, "How is Mr. Beckman doing? Can my daughters go in now for a visit?"

"Check with the floor nurse before you go in," she said, then turned her attention back to what she had been writing.

We followed Mama down a maze of hallways. All the walls were white, and the green-and-black-tiled floors shined. Nurses walked the halls, wearing starched white uniforms and thick-soled white shoes.

I'd never visited anyone in the hospital before. Everyone talked quietly. Open doors revealed sick people lying in bed. It felt like an intrusion to see their pain and helplessness. I tried not to glance in as we passed by the rooms.

"Wait here." Mama entered a doorway, then came out and motioned us to follow.

I held my breath and entered.

Daddy lay in a bed next to a window. The Venetian blinds were open, and beyond the window, people on the sidewalk hustled by as if everything was normal.

The top of the bed was slightly raised, two pillows propped up his head and shoulders. Face ashen, eyes closed, an oxygen mask covered his mouth and nose. Tiny tubes dripped clear liquid through needles stuck in his arm. I hated the needles. They looked painful, but Daddy lay there seemingly unaware of them.

Veronica and I timidly approached him.

"Hi, Daddy," Veronica said.

I reached over to touch his hand, to hold it. His icy limp fingers couldn't wrap around mine and hold hands back. Daddy had always been so strong. I bit my lip and tried not to sob.

Mama sat in one of the two chairs in the room. She began telling Daddy about the neighbors, acting as if nothing was wrong and he understood everything she said.

Veronica and I took turns sitting in the other chair. After we'd sat for a while, she asked, "Can we go to the cafeteria, Mama?"

"Okay, just be quiet. They'll throw you out if you make too much noise."

"We'll be quiet," Veronica said.

The room felt like a straitjacket. I felt guilty but could hardly wait to leave. We wandered the hospital halls until we found the cafeteria. It smelled of stale coffee and icky, overcooked food. Tired looking nurses glided in and out of the room. Nursing sick and dying people would be dreadful. I'd much rather take care of horses.

Mama had given Veronica money if we got hungry, and she asked, "Do you want anything?"

"Maybe a soda."

While we sat silently drinking sodas, I noticed Veronica wore a blue sweater I'd never seen before. "Where'd you get that sweater?" I asked.

"It's Jenny Lee's."

The sweater would fit as tight as a glove on Jenny Lee but loosely draped my sister's slender shoulders. I felt the sweater's soft yarn and asked, "Do you like Jenny Lee? She's so weird."

Veronica lifted her lips from the straw in mid-sip. "Yeah, she's different."

"Not different," I said. "She's a juvenile delinquent and blabs about being in juvie. It's embarrassing."

Tilting her head as if considering, Veronica looked at the ceiling, then lowered her gaze to stare at the coke machine. "Her life is awful. She hates her stepfather and blames her mother for not kicking him out."

"What happened with her stepfather?"

Veronica gave me an it's-for-me-to-know-and-you-to-find-out look. "Well, it's sad." Sighing, she brushed back a strand of hair. "She doesn't have anyone who cares much about her. Underneath all the tough talk, she needs a friend."

"What about her grandma? She seems to care. Why hang around with a juvie girl. You've always had nice friends. Good thing she won't be going to school with us."

Veronica set her soda on the table, leaned forward, and rolled her eyes. "Friends? You mean the bunch I used to hang out with? They always made me feel they were judging me all the time. Like if I said the wrong thing, wore the wrong clothes, I'd be out of the group."

I shrugged and said, "Judged by everyone? I understand wanting a friend that likes you for yourself and all that, but still, Jenny Lee? Talk about bad clothes and makeup. She looks like a cross between the bride of Frankenstein and a trollop."

Veronica nodded. "Yeah. She could use a few fashion tips, but she likes me. She'd do anything for me. I don't want to hurt her feelings."

"Honestly," I said, "you'd be doing her a big favor if you did. You should discourage her from stealing too. It could get her back in juvie and get you into trouble, too."

The warm room and smell of yucky food and old coffee got to us. We left the cafeteria to explore the quiet halls and found the emergency room where Daddy had been brought after his accident. I looked for Trudy's mom but didn't see her. In the emergency waiting area, we sat in stiff chairs for a while, dreading to return to Daddy's room.

Eventually, we wandered back. Nothing had changed. Daddy still lay with his eyes closed. Mama still sat at his bedside, with her sweater folded on her lap. She gazed at us with a blank, weary expression and said, "If you're ready, you can go home, then come back and pick me up this afternoon."

Veronica asked, "What time do you want me back here?"

"About 4 o'clock. By then, the doctor will have made his rounds, and I'll have had a chance to talk to him."

I squeezed Daddy's limp hand and kissed Mama before I left.

Relieved to get out of that room, I hurried down the hall and out of the hospital. On the drive home, Veronica pulled the car over to the side of the road and parked. She leaned her head against the steering wheel and sobbed. Her tears made me cry too. We sat there together as cars passed, sniffing and crying.

Then she raised her head, leaned back against the seat, and stared out the windshield, trying to control her tears. She sniffed and wiped her eyes with the back of her fist. "Didn't Daddy look awful? He looks dead. Don't know if I can stand going back into his room."

I reached over and grasped her hand. "Let's pray for Daddy."

Veronica sat stiffly, closed her eyes, and didn't say anything about depending on the doctors while I mumbled a short prayer. After a few minutes, she started the engine, and we drove home with the stink of burning trash drifting in the open windows.

Chapter Eighteen
Good-bye

The day we visited Daddy, Veronica drove us home and then later went back to the hospital to pick up Mama. When they got back that evening, Mama silently sat at the kitchen table staring out the window.

Veronica had to tell me.

"Daddy died."

We quietly sat with Mama.

I bit my lip to keep from bawling and waited for someone to say something. My chest ached until I thought my heart would explode. Then my sobs burst out.

Veronica started to cry too.

Mama wiped her eyes with the back of her hand, then stood and went to her bedroom.

My sister and I both continued to sob until Veronica sniffed back her tears and said, "I hope Mama doesn't get drunk. That's all we need."

The next morning, Mama looked ragged but appeared sober. She made coffee and smoked cigarette after cigarette. Finally, she emptied the ashtray into the trash and said, "Your daddy needs something nice to wear."

The importance of Daddy wearing new clothes to his funeral seemed strange. Even so, we all went to Penny's Department Store and bought him a new dark blue suit, the kind he'd wear to a party. We went to the funeral parlor to give it to the creepy funeral director, who also needed a new suit. The way his hung on him, he must have lost twenty pounds since he'd bought it.

Veronica and I helped Mama pick out a casket. While showing them to us, the undertaker spoke softly as if worried he'd wake the dead. We had a choice of oak, bronze, or brocade-covered pine. Mama said we should choose one Daddy would want, which seemed stupid because he wouldn't have wanted any of them.

*****

Even though it was summer, morning fog shrouded the sun. My sister started a fire in the old wood stove and huddled close to its warmth. I sat with my elbows propped on the table, resting my chin in my hand, studying the swirling patterns in the yellow Formica.

Mama sat across from me. Dark circles puffed under her bloodshot eyes, and her face sagged like a Halloween mask. Since Daddy died, she'd been drunk, but she seemed sober now.

I hoped she could get through the funeral today without a drink.

The refrigerator hummed, two white dishtowels hung neatly together on the towel bar, and last night's dirty dishes were still piled in the sink. It seemed strange nothing in the kitchen looked different, yet everything had changed. It was hard to believe Daddy would never be coming home.

I got up and opened the refrigerator, filled with two berry pies, a loaf of homemade bread Mrs. Barr had brought over, a casserole, and a huge bowl of potato salad from Ben's mom.

"We can't eat all this," I said.

Mama's hand shook as she poured another cup of coffee. "The neighbors will need something to eat when they come over after the service."

The funeral would be at eleven. The only sound in the house was water splashing into the clawfoot tub as we took turns bathing. When it was time to get dressed, the fog had lifted, and the tree limb outside my window cast shadows in my bedroom as I slipped on my gloomiest dress.

Mama insisted we ride in Daddy's black Buick to the funeral. Veronica drove past the movie theater in Arroyo Viejo, where a few days ago, my only worry was kissing boys. Now, we were going to bury Daddy.

The inside of the church reeked of flowers. The cross above the pulpit loomed over Daddy's bronze casket. Surrounded by colorful summery bouquets, its lid was open. The undertaker seated us in the front pew where I could see Daddy's nose protruding from the coffin.

Soft music played in the background while people found their seats. Trudy and her mom sat across the aisle in the front row with Ben and his mom. Mr. and Mrs. Barr and Jenny Lee's grandmother sat there too. I didn't see Jenny Lee.

The preacher came in and stood behind the pulpit. Even though he'd never met him, he said Daddy had been a good man and father. That Daddy had lived a good life, and we would all see him again in heaven.

No talk of hell today.

A woman sang the "Old Rugged Cross," which made us sniff and cry. Then our neighbors meandered by the casket to say good-bye to Daddy for the last time.

After they had all filed out the door, Mama said, "It's time for us to say good-bye too."

With a grim expression, the funeral director helped Mama stand and watched while she and Veronica gazed down at Daddy.

When I went to the funeral parlor with Mama to make the arrangements, I hadn't gone in with her and Veronica to view Daddy's body. I was afraid. I knew if I saw him in the casket, his death would be real. The way it became real how sick he was when I saw him lying in that horrible hospital bed.

Now, I still did not want to see Daddy. I intended to close my eyes when I walked past his coffin.

I stood back and waited, realizing I'd never see him again. Should I go against my feelings and look? Every inch of me didn't want to, but I might be sorry if I didn't. It was my last chance to see his face.

I wiped my nose, choked back tears, and stepped closer to the casket.

With eyes serenely closed and hands folded on his chest as if in prayer, his head rested on a white satin pillow. The new suit fit perfectly, except the white shirt looked a bit tight around his neck. He didn't actually look dead. Except in life, I'd never seen him wear a suit and tie or sleep on satin.

I sniffled. "Good-bye, Daddy."

Behind me, Mama blew her nose and cleared her throat. "Let's go."

Her hand was cold as we walked outside into the bright sunshine. We joined our neighbors and followed pallbearers toting Daddy's casket to the graveyard. They carefully placed it over an open grave. We sat in front of the casket, and I tried not to look into the deep rectangular pit awaiting Daddy's coffin. The preacher said more prayers, and then our neighbors milled around talking and telling Mama how sorry they were.

We sat there silently until everyone left, and then Mama said, "We better go home. People will be coming to pay their respects."

After the funeral, the neighbors brought more food and gathered in our small living room and kitchen. Our table overflowed with casseroles, pies, baked ham, and salads. Jenny Lee and Veronica sat outside on the front porch while I stood near the doorway between the kitchen and living room, where I could watch everyone.

Mrs. Barr sat on our green couch, balancing a coffee cup in one hand and a piece of pie on her knees. Beside her, a pair of white gloves lay on a black purse. While she and Ben's mom talked, Ben stood next to them, looking stiff and uncomfortable in a white shirt and tie. Trudy sat with her mom, but I didn't want to talk to her. Besides, she seemed more interested in Ben than in me. And he probably noticed how her snug sweater showed off her bra size.

When we'd gotten home from the funeral, Mama had gone into her room. Now, she came into the kitchen. I could tell she'd been drinking. Mr. Barr stood to give Mama his chair. She started to sit but staggered and fell flat on her rump.

Everyone rushed over, and Mr. Barr helped Mama to her feet. "Mrs. Beckman, are you all right?"

"Of course, I'm not all right," Mama shrieked. "My husband is dead. How can I be all right?"

Oh, gads! My drunken mother created a scene in front of all our neighbors. I wished I were invisible. While everyone helped Mama into a chair, I slipped out the back door and sprinted up the hill trail to hide in the barn until everyone went home. I couldn't face the neighbors, especially Trudy and Ben.

When they heard me, the mares and Chaos came. I sat on the haystack and watched them eat. It was peaceful here, no unhappy Mama, no nosey neighbors, no one staring at me.

Climbing down from the haystack, I talked to Babyface and groomed her golden coat with a stiff brush. "Daddy was buried today. Except for the suit, he looked the same as always. It was horrible. It wasn't really Daddy. What will we do without him? With Mama drinking so much, I can't count on her."

My eyes filled with tears. Ever since I could remember, Mama had a drinking problem. When she drank, things turned topsy-turvy, and uproar ruled. Once, when I was about four, Mama took me to a coffee shop, bought me a milkshake, and then left me there while she went to a bar next door.

It was hot. A fan swished overhead, trying to keep the warm restaurant cool. My sweaty bare legs stuck to the big booth's red plastic seat. I finished my shake, but she hadn't returned. I sat for what seemed like hours.

Scared Mama had left me forever, I covered my face with my hands to hide my dribbling tears. The waitress could tell I was bawling and said, "Don't worry, your mama will be back soon."

She kept giving me ice cream until I ate so much my tongue froze. Daddy found me crying in the coffee shop, carried me to his Buick, and drove me home.

I wasn't four anymore, but that memory left an ache in my chest. I pressed my wet face against Babyface's strong neck and told her, "Mama might want to move into town and get rid of you. Without you and my barn hideout or any friends, what am I going to do?"

A noise startled Chaos. I turned, and Trudy stood behind me.

"I didn't hear you come in." I peered at the ground, sniffed back tears, and wiped my runny nose with the back of my hand. My face must have looked a mess.

"I'm sorry about your dad."

I stared at her painted red toenails and sandaled feet. How much had she heard me tell Babyface? Now she'd have another reason to laugh.

Trudy's fingers entwined Babyface's mane. "Would you like to come to an Alateen meeting at my church? A group of kids has just started meeting once a week to share our problems."

She placed her hand on my shoulder. "You see, my dad's an alcoholic.

He goes to meetings, too. They've helped him stop drinking. Do you think your mother would like to go to one? With your father gone, it'll be hard for her. She'll feel sad and might need someone to talk to."

Surprised by what she told me, I said, "Your dad drinks?"

Trudy looked out the barn door and sighed. "He's stopped drinking, but he's still an alcoholic. The meetings Mom and I go to help families of alcoholics."

"What happens at the meetings?" I asked, even though I'd be too embarrassed to go and tell awful things about my family in front of a room full of strangers.

"We talk. That's all. It helps to find out you're not alone. That you have friends who care."

I felt weepy. "You want to be my friend? I thought you didn't like me because I smoked with Jenny Lee, and you laughed when Babyface almost ruined my new saddle."

Trudy smiled. "Of course, I want to be your friend. I didn't mean to be so critical, but true friends discourage you when you're doing something wrong." She shook her head and looked down. "I shouldn't have laughed. I envied you getting a new saddle, but I'm glad your father bought it for you. Especially now. You'll always think of him when you ride Babyface."

"It's a remembrance." I gulped, then started crying again.

Trudy took my hand. "Come on. Let's go back to your house. Everyone must miss you."

Back at the house, Ben sat on the cement steps. When he saw us coming down the hill trail, he stood and climbed up to meet us. His green eyes probed mine. "I was worried and wondered where you were."

"I had to feed the horses," I lied.

Trudy's hand squeezed mine. The three of us sat crowded together on the crumbly steps, chatted about horses and school, with no mention of Mama or her *problem.*

Veronica and Jenny Lee joined us. We began telling Daddy stories. I told about hunting jackrabbits with Daddy on the cotton farm and how he'd planned to help me train Chaos. The stories made me sad and happy at the same time.

Chapter Nineteen
Beginnings

When Daddy was alive, Mama went on an occasional drinking binge for a day or two. For months she'd be fine, then something would set her off. I never knew when it would happen. That was why I never invited anyone to our house.

If we were lucky, when we got home from school, she'd be passed out on the couch. Otherwise, she'd argue with Daddy and us. Maybe she'd complain the house looked like a hog pen. She'd stagger around cleaning and slam the vacuum against the walls and furniture. Once, she mopped the floor like a madwoman, water sloshed all over, and she slipped, fell, and broke her wrist.

Daddy never lost his temper when she acted awful. He'd talk to her as if she were a little girl. He'd convince her she needed to rest. He'd tuck her into bed and then would make dinner for us.

Now, without Daddy here to act as her keeper, Mama drank every day. She often retreated to her room, wouldn't come out to eat or answer her door when I knocked. Though she didn't open it, the door wasn't locked, so I went in anyway. I found Daddy's clothing strewn around the room and Mama lying in bed, curled up in a ball.

Sometimes she slept all day, woke up in the middle of the night, and wandered through the house, rummaging in the closets. Or she sat at the kitchen table looking through photo albums, crying. She wouldn't bother to go to the front door when Mrs. Barr knocked. Veronica or I had to go to the door and thank her for the fruit and vegetables she'd brought from her garden.

The worst was when she decided to make dinner. She would chop Mrs. Barr's vegetables into minute inedible bits, fling potato peelings on the floor, shuck corn and send husks flying. She would put stuff on the stove to cook, forget about it, and leave it to burn. I worried she'd hack off a finger, fall and break her neck, or burn the house down while cooking or smoking in bed. If I tried to help her, she got angry and wanted to argue.

Veronica and I did our best to avoid her. We escaped the house. I doubted Mama even noticed we were gone.

I usually went up to the barn to feed and confer with the horses about my problems. One morning, Ben had also hiked up to his pasture next door. He waved at me from the other side of the fence. Trudy must have spied us from her perch because she showed up just as Ben squeezed through the barbed wire. We went into the barn so he could admire the tractor again. We started talking about stage robbers and decided to hunt for their hidden loot.

First, Ben got a shovel from his dad's tool shed, and we began to search inside the barn. He drew squares in the dirt the way Mr. Buck had shown him. Then he started to dig while Trudy and I pointed.

Moldy smelling dirt, encrusted with a zillion years of mummified manure, flaked off in layers like cardboard. Ben chipped away at it for about an hour but only found a broken horseshoe, a rusty hinge, and some spent cartridges.

By the time Ben decided to quit, he had thoroughly raked the barn floor. After he left to go home, the mares and Chaos inspected the heap of dried manure Ben had piled outside the door. They moseyed into their clean barn, and while they ate, Chaos butted her mama's udder and nursed.

While we watched the filly, Trudy invited me to go to a meeting again.

I still loathed the idea of going. Mama said family problems were to be kept in the family, and nice people never hung out their dirty laundry. Undressed truth didn't appeal to me. It scared me to let people inside. Talking about Mama's drinking picked at the scab of my hurt, opened the wound, and made it bleed. It was easier to cover the sore with a Band-Aid, pretend everything was fine, swallow my humiliation and fears, and act as if I were a pod person without emotions like a character in the movie *The Invasion of the Body Snatchers*.

"Do I have to talk?" I asked.

Trudy must have sensed my reluctance. To convince me, she said, "You don't have to, but no one ever repeats what's said at a meeting. It's part of the code."

"I'll think about it," I said, still not intending to go, planning instead to just tell my problems to the horses.

A few days later, when Trudy's mom found out Mama was depressed and drinking, she came over and encouraged her to get out of bed. Then they sat in the kitchen, poured many cups of coffee, and Trudy's mom held Mama's hand and listened. Mama cried, which must have made her feel better because later after Trudy's mom left, she ate the dinner Veronica cooked. It was our first family meal together since Daddy died.

But Mama continued to drink, moped around the house, and became sadder and sadder. So to figure out how to make Mama happier, I got up my nerve and asked to go with Trudy and her mom to an Alateen meeting.

After I decided to go, so did Veronica, although at first, I suspected she went because she thought Trudy's older brother would be there. Then Jenny Lee decided to go because of Veronica. It snowballed.

Trudy's mother, the group leader, drove us to a small building behind the sinner's church, where the meeting was being held. Inside, tucked in the corner of one large green room, was a small kitchen complete with sink, stove, and refrigerator, which was probably why the place smelled like spaghetti sauce. Chairs and a long table were shoved against one wall. We all helped drag them to the center of the room, opened the folding chairs, and placed them around the table.

Trudy's mom set out a plate of cookies, and in about ten minutes, five kids showed up and joined us at the table. Trudy and Veronica sat on each side of me, and Jenny Lee sat next to Veronica. As Trudy led us in "The Serenity Prayer" in a firm voice, I stumbled over the words:

God grant me the serenity
To accept the things I cannot change,
Courage to change the things I can,
And wisdom to know the difference.

Trudy's mom explained many families had problems with alcohol and told us about the twelve steps, the twelve traditions, and how anonymity was the tradition's spiritual foundation, which was fine with me. The last thing I wanted to do was to tell people about going to a meeting because my mother was an alcoholic.

Since the Alateen program had recently been formed for teenagers, everyone was new to the group. Trudy's mom encouraged us to talk about anything we wanted.

We munched cookies and looked anywhere but at each other. Then a dark-haired girl about my age, with her hands clasped so tightly together her knuckles were white, said, "I've been attending Al-Anon meetings with my mother. I'm glad teenagers have a group now."

"I'm excited we have our own meetings now, too," Trudy said. "Things changed at our house after my dad joined AA. It's helped him. When he used to drink, it was bad."

The AA meetings sounded good. If Mama joined, would it help her stop drinking, too?

Almost in a whisper, a skinny boy nodded his curly head and said, "When my dad goes on a bender, sometimes he's gone for days. We don't know where he is, and my mom worries he's been in an accident. It hurts deep in my gut that when he drinks, we don't exist."

"Yeah," Jenny Lee piped in. "When my mom's drunk, she couldn't care less about me. Even sober, she doesn't care much until I create problems for her. It's only when I do something bad that she notices I'm alive."

Jenny Lee grimaced, and her overly made-up eyes turned fierce. "All she cares about is my drunken stepfather. She should throw him out. When she's not home, he can't keep his hands off me. He's a real creep. He makes me feel like dirt. God, how I hate him."

Jenny Lee knotted her hands into fists and blinked back tears. My sister patted her shoulder, and Jenny Lee reached up and squeezed Veronica's hand.

This encouraged my sister to talk. Staring at the coffee-stained table, Veronica inhaled deeply, held the huge breath a second, and then slowly exhaled and said, "It was hard enough dealing with my mother when my father was alive. Now that he's gone, her drinking has gotten worse. She gets drunk every day, staggers around the house, or passes out, dead to the world. I'm tired of worrying about her, and I'm sick of being stuck with the responsibility of being my mother's mother. It's not fair!"

She sniffed and wiped her nose with the back of her hand. "Even sober, she's never there for me either. When I became a cheerleader or get good grades, she never acts proud of me."

Veronica's eyes teared up, and Jenny Lee reached over and hugged her shoulder to console her. Even if Jenny Lee was kooky, she knew how hard it was to live with an alcoholic. She'd experienced the same kind of dreadful scenes, disappointments, and uproar in her life that Veronica had -- and worse. Her friendship and support comforted my sister. If she wanted her for a friend, it was all right with me, no matter how wacky Jenny Lee was.

No one spoke.

Trudy looked at me as if it was my turn to talk.

The silent room and Trudy's blue staring eyes made me uneasy and prodded me into overcoming my embarrassment about speaking. When I did, my words rushed out. "Ever since I can remember, my mother drank. I try not to upset her, but I never know for sure what might set her off on a drinking spree. Since Daddy died, she drinks every day. She cares more about whiskey than she does about me. Gads, I miss Daddy. I feel like an abandoned orphan. It was like when he died, Mama died, too. Now I don't have anyone to take care of me."

I stopped rambling and gulped back tears. Sucking in my breath, I stammered, "I, uh, I try to be good and make Mama happy so that she won't drink. It doesn't matter what I do. She drinks anyway."

"It's not their kids' fault alcoholics drink," Trudy said. "We can't change our parents, but we can change how we feel about ourselves."

Trudy talked about what she'd learned attending Al-Anon meetings with her mom. She said my mother was responsible for her drinking, not me, and a parent's alcohol abuse could injure children in ways they didn't always understand. Parents were supposed to take care of their kids and keep them safe, but when parents drank, children had to fend for themselves.

Instead of going on and on about my problems, I listened in the way Joseph said to do with the horses and began to understand how hurt and helpless I felt. I realized it was okay to feel angry.

All at once, I began to cry.

In a quaky voice, Veronica said, "I love you guys," and started bawling, too. So did Trudy and Jenny Lee.

I felt humiliated but crying seemed to help get rid of some of the awful ache squeezing my heart since Daddy died. It was strange. I went to the meeting to learn how to help Mama, but instead, I found help for myself.

Chapter Twenty
Changes

It was late afternoon when Jenny Lee came over to our house, and she and Veronica disappeared into her bedroom. The closed door creaked when I leaned my ear against it.

"I know that's you, Winna," Veronica said. "Quit eavesdropping. Come in and close the door."

I went in. They sat on the floor facing each other, pow-wow style. Veronica pointed at the empty spot beside her and said, "Sit."

I sat as told, and not to miss any good stuff, I leaned forward to listen. It took me a second to realize Jenny Lee looked different. Without makeup, her scrubbed face looked younger. Her eyes were puffy. She'd been crying.

Jenny Lee finger-combed her ratty looking hair, inhaled, and exhaled a loud sigh. "Trudy's mom called me after the meeting last night. She said I should tell Grandma about the problem with my stepfather."

She looked down at her tattooed hands, sniffed, and bit her nude lip. "Man, oh man, when I did, Grandma called the cops. I never told her before 'cause I figured it would stir up all kinds of hell. Boy, was I right. Mom got mad and accused me of lying. Said not to come home. I should stay with Grandma."

Jenny Lee covered her face with her hands and busted out bawling.

Gads, Jenny Lee's mother was a real dud. Compared to her, Mama was almost an angel.

"It'll be okay," Veronica said, patting Jenny Lee's shoulder.

Jenny Lee gulped back sobs and nodded. "Grandma wants me to finish high school. Guess I'll go this fall if the school will have me."

"That'll be good," Veronica said. "You wanted to live here. It's all for the best."

Had my sister's brain gone south for the summer? I felt sorry for Jenny Lee. Even so, her living across the road forever didn't sound like the best to me.

Jenny Lee shrugged and took a deep breath. "Grandma said I had to stay out of trouble and made me swear on the Bible I would."

I hoped Jenny Lee meant it. Maybe if she got a horse, it would help.

*****

Veronica began spending a lot of time over at Jenny Lee's. I visited the horses, and Chaos and I became friends. She liked to be brushed and get her rear end scratched. She nibbled at my hair and clothes. She never bit *too* hard.

I spent hours riding horseback with Ben and Trudy, and we went to a few of Ben's baseball games. After a late ball game or Alateen meeting, I stayed overnight at Trudy's. I would have liked to have stayed more often, but number 71 on Mama's ladies' list was: don't wear out your welcome.

One afternoon, I happened to be home when someone knocked on the door. When I opened it, I expected to see Mrs. Barr. Instead, I was surprised Joseph stood on the front porch.

"Oh, Joseph, hello."

He took off his hat and gazed down at his polished black boots. "I'm sorry about your daddy."

I didn't know what to say except, "Thank you."

He kept looking down and fiddling with his hat brim.

"I love the saddle Daddy bought," I said. "It's so perfect."

He raised his milky brown eyes. "Glad ya like it. I have this here tiny halter. Thought ya could use it on your filly. That is if ya don't already got one."

"No. I don't. That would be great. It's time to halter train her. She's not afraid of me anymore. Want to see her? She's a beauty."

"Sure would. Hold on a minute."

Joseph got the halter out of his truck. As we hiked up the hill trail, I felt sad. Daddy should be helping me halter train Chaos.

The horses noticed us walking toward the barn and followed. While Joseph watched me throw them hay, Chaos raised her head and eyed the stranger. It hardly took a minute for her to sidle over to Joseph, sniff the halter he held, and let him scratch behind her ear.

"Looks like she's ready for more training," Joseph said and handed me the halter. "First, rub her with the halter to get her used to the feel of it."

Chaos was shedding. Under tuffs of baby hair, her new coat looked sleek and grayish brown. I stroked her back and side with the leather halter. She turned her head and sniffed the oiled leather, then tried to chew it. I opened the noseband wide, and she stuck her muzzle inside. I slipped it on and off her a few times. Then she let me buckle it on.

Joseph laughed. "She's a dandy. Since I'm here to help ya, might as well go ahead and teach her to lead."

Babyface's halter and lead rope hung on a nail inside the barn. Joseph retrieved the rope and gave it to me. "All ya gotta do is loop this here lead rope around her rump and pull a bit to encourage her to take a step."

Chaos didn't seem to mind when I snapped the lead on her halter. Things changed when I wrapped the rope around her rump and pulled. Instead of going forward, she kicked and backed up. I followed her as she stepped backward. She stopped backing but looked a little wild-eyed.

"You done right," Joseph said. "Don't let loose of the rope. She'll get used to it."

We stood there a few minutes, and the wild look in her eye softened.

"Okey-dokey," Joseph said. "Let's try 'er again. This time keep a steady pressure against her rump with the rope. Don't follow when she backs up."

I pulled steadily on her butt rope. Again, she tried to step back.

Joseph said, "Hang on to that rope 'til she steps forward."

Chaos leaned her weight against the rope. I kept hold. She felt as if she weighed over a hundred pounds. My arms ached when she finally quit sitting back and took a step forward.

"There ya go. That's the way it's done," Joseph said and walked over to scratch Chaos. "Lesson's over. Now, give her a good brushin'. She'll do better next time."

Chaos stood quietly when I took the lead rope from around her backside.

Joseph handed me the brush. "Anytime ya want help trainin' your filly, just ask. I'll come over."

"Thank you for the halter and your help," I said.

He waved goodbye and left me alone in the barn with the horses.

As I brushed Chaos, she nibbled my shirttail, and I slipped the halter on her a few more times. I wished Daddy were here to see how pretty and smart she is and how well her training was going. If he were watching from heaven, he'd be pleased Joseph offered to help me with the filly. Like Daddy, Joseph knew tons about training horses. Maybe I wouldn't have to buy Professor Beery's horsemanship manual, after all.

Chapter Twenty-one
School Starts

About a week before school started, Veronica and I stood at the sink washing dishes when Mama came into the kitchen. She sat at the table, smoked, and stared into space. She seemed unaware of us as we talked about Jenny Lee's problems, and the new horse her grandmother had bought for her.

Mama looked at us with weary eyes. "Jenny Lee's grandmother says the Alateen meetings have helped Jenny Lee. Have they helped you girls, too?"

Veronica and I exchanged a glance and nodded.

Mama began wringing her hands. "It's been a rough go since your daddy died. I've got to get a grip. I can't keep going the way I have been since..." She lowered her gaze, heaved a sigh, and stilled her hands. "With your daddy gone, I know you need a sober mother. Trudy's father invited me to go with him to an Alcoholics Anonymous meeting. I think I should go."

When Trudy's dad picked Mama up about 6:00 in the evening to go to the AA meeting, she was sober for the first time in ages. She came home later with a handful of pamphlets. I made hot chocolate and sat at the table with her as she skimmed through them. Every so often, she'd read an important passage out loud.

Mama stopped reading, then with a furrowed brow, she looked up and said, "Don't worry, Winna. With God's help, I'm going to stay sober."

She had made promises before she hadn't kept. This time, I prayed God *would* help her.

*****

Mama held the front door open and said, "Hurry, or you'll miss your bus."

I grabbed my new blue sweater and said, "Bye, Mama."

Veronica and I rushed outside and down our long driveway to the bus stop. I wanted to get there before the bus arrived so the kids wouldn't see me running like an idiot to catch it. I didn't want to look like a complete dope on my first day at school.

Ben and Trudy waited at the end of the driveway. It was so cold Trudy's breath came out in a puff cloud when she said, "Hi."

Ben's green eyes lit up when he smiled at me. The most handsomest, nicest boy ever, he still made my heart patter like crazy every time he got a tiny bit too close. I still waited for my first kiss. I probably needed to act more ladylike to attract him. When I first met him, his good looks impressed me. After getting to know him, I realized he was more than just cute. Even though he'd found out I was a ninth grader, we'd stayed friends. He was kind and knew how to be a friend to a girl.

Jenny Lee's grandmother must have taken her shopping. A red shirtwaist dress flapped around her knees as she raced across the road to join us. Though still black, her hair curled under in a pageboy and looked like a normal person's. She'd toned down her makeup too. I hoped my sister had told her to keep her trap shut about being in juvie, at least on the first day.

I barely had time to pull on my sweater before the high school bus arrived and groaned to a stop. Its twin doors swung open, and warm air swooshed out. Trudy and I climbed the steps and squeezed down the narrow aisle until we found a seat together. Veronica and Jenny Lee sat behind us. Ben walked to the back to sit in the very last row with a group of noisy boys wearing baseball caps.

"I could hardly sleep last night," I said.

Trudy's long ponytail bounced as she nodded. "Me neither. The first day of school is the worst. Too bad we don't have any classes together. Let's meet in the cafeteria at lunch."

I pulled a wrinkled paper out of my binder to show her. "I found the map I'd sketched of our archeological dig in my pocket. I redrew it and added the barn in our treasure hunt grid."

Trudy studied my sketch. "It's good. You should color it in."

I shook my head. "It's not even close to perfect. The measurements are wrong. I'm taking an art class. Maybe I can learn how to draw it right."

"No, your map really is good."

I knew she was trying to be nice. That was Trudy's way. When I said Mama might want to move into town and that I wouldn't be able to keep the horses if we left our apple farm. She told her mom, who said it would be okay for Babyface, Snafu, and Chaos to stay in Blackie's pasture.

Then Mr. Barr offered to help Mama take care of the apple orchard.

"I sure would appreciate it," she said. "I'm going to do my best to keep the farm. Don't need to make any more changes now. There's been too many in our lives already."

I agreed -- too many changes.

Except not all the changes were bad. Veronica and I didn't argue so much, and Trudy and I had become best friends, even though I thought she had a crush on Ben.

I still didn't tell every feeling or thought that popped into my head. One thing I hadn't told Trudy was that I admired her for admitting she envied my saddle or that I envied how pretty she was, even with those awful braces. Just because I didn't tell her didn't make me a big liar.

Another thing Trudy didn't need to know was when Mama had forgotten to give back Mr. Buck's bayonet, I'd hidden it under my mattress. Veronica didn't need to know, either. My sister knew how to get my goat and would say God hated a thief, or I had sinned, or something nasty like that.

I didn't care what she said. It wasn't exactly stealing. I couldn't part with the bayonet. I didn't want Mama to give it back yet. It reminded me of Daddy and the day we moved here.

It perturbed me God didn't answer my prayers to let Daddy stay here with us. Did God even listen to my prayers? I had no real evidence, except Mama was still sober and going to AA meetings. I had new friends, not the kind who stared down their snouts at me. I had not just one but three horses, and we had the world's nicest neighbors.

Still, it wasn't fair Daddy died. He was a good father, and even though he didn't go to church, I knew now he was in heaven. I loved and missed him, and he probably missed us, too.

Mama always said, "Life isn't fair."

She was right. Life was unfair and as unpredictable as riding Babyface. Sometimes I had a hard time keeping my balance, and I got bumps and bruises when I fell off. Even so, people could be big-hearted. I had to trust and believe, no matter what, things would work out, and as Daddy said, "Keep climbing back on."

About Alateen

In 1957, Al-Anon created Alateen, a program for young people that caters to teenagers' emotional and social needs. Like Al-Anon, Alateen operates by holding meetings through local chapters. Teenagers can get together at churches, businesses, or even someone's home. The meetings provide teenagers who have family members who drink or who may have a drinking problem themselves an opportunity to discuss their problems with their peers and "vent" about drinking-related issues. By sharing experiences and admitting there is a problem, teens can overcome their issues and the many difficulties living with a drinking household and perhaps gain the strength and courage to help others.

About Wanda Snow Porter

Wanda Snow Porter writes books for the family: novels, non-fiction, and picture books. She grew up on a small farm on the California coast and learned to love nature and animals while riding horseback on land once part of an old Mexican rancho. An avid horsewoman, she has owned and trained horses all her life, both western and English, earning a Bronze Medal Riders Award from the United States Dressage Federation. She loves being a grandmother and enjoys bird watching, photography, and being a docent at Rancho Nipomo's historic Dana Adobe.

Books by the Author

Fiction
Spurs for Jose
Remedy
Riding Babyface
Ordinary Miracles

Non-fiction
Voyages of No Return:
Mutiny on the HMS Bounty and Beyond

Picture Books
Capturing Time
Christmas Kitten
Horses Change Coats
Has God

Made in United States
North Haven, CT
05 February 2022

15692113R00071